Jump

Jump

a novel by

Ginger Rue

Tricycle Press
Berkeley

For my parents & brother.

chapter one

*L*ook, Brinkley, I understand that you don't want to talk to me, but you're going to have to say something at some point." Brinkley Harper had been sitting in the therapist's office for nearly ten minutes without saying a word. The therapist paused before continuing, "Why don't you start by telling me why you're here?"

"Because my parents think being expelled from Story High won't look so hot on my college resume," Brinkley said.

This was an understatement.

Story High, named for Supreme Court Justice Joseph Story, had an impeccable reputation with the area's finest families, though it also bused in undesirables from middle-class neighborhoods to bolster its claims of socioeconomic diversity. Having an expulsion from Story on one's record was practically a one-way to some State U.

Brinkley leaned back in her chair and crossed her arms. "I drive all the way over here to your dumpy little office, do my time with you until you sign off on my forms, and the principal gets to save face, pretend he really threw the book at me."

"Don't you think it was generous of the principal to allow you to attend off-campus counseling instead of expelling you? From what I understand, he did bend the school's zero-tolerance policy for your sake."

"Yeah. I'm sure his willingness to work out a compromise has nothing to do my dad's being on the board and the fact that my family funded the new auditorium." Brinkley narrowed her eyes. "Where'd they dig you up, anyway? I don't see any degrees on your wall."

The counselor smiled. "I don't believe in crass displays—of education or of wealth," she said.

Brinkley slipped off her Louboutins and tucked her legs under herself to get comfortable. She certainly saw no outward signs of wealth in this excuse for an office. It was a dingy room with lots of books. The only window was open, and every so often a breeze would stir a collection of prisms and wind chimes. The desk was a study in disorganization, much like the therapist's wild curls. She wore a tie-dyed kurta, jeans, and clogs—the ensemble looked like a combination of nineties grunge and sixties flower child.

"What did you say your name was—Dr. what?"

"I didn't. You needn't call me by a courtesy title. I feel it sets up an unnecessary barrier. You may call me Irirangi."

Brinkley smirked. "Seriously, I'm cool with a barrier, Doc."

Irirangi looked at her gently. "You still haven't told me why you're here."

"Yes, I did. My dad arranged it to keep my slot at Story."

"And are you proud of your father's power?"

"I dunno. Hadn't really thought about it. So, can we get this over with? Just sign the stupid form that says I'm done, and then we can all go about our usual lives."

"Brinkley, the principal sent you to me for a reason. What was that reason?"

"Oh, that. Well, apparently, I'm a terrible, scary bully." Brinkley laughed.

"And are you?"

"No."

"Then why would the principal think so?"

"Because some girls are jealous of me . . . like it's *my* fault nobody likes them. If a few girls leave Story to go somewhere else, that's their choice. I didn't *make* them."

"A few girls? I believe the exact number was four. That's quite a few."

Brinkley shrugged. "Well, it's not like they all left at once."

"Isn't the important part *why* they left?"

"Look, it's not my fault they couldn't handle their inferiority. They were just jealous because I'm prettier, richer, more popular, and because I have the hottest boyfriend. I can't help it if they're not as good as me."

"That's interesting. They're blaming you for their problems."

"Yes."

"That's not a very effective way to deal with an issue, blaming other people."

"Hey, lady, that's what I'm screamin'," Brinkley said as she stretched and yawned.

"So the fact that this . . ." Irirangi flipped a page in her notes and found a name. "Ella Gilbert's parents pulled her out of school and sent her to a clinic for eating disorders has nothing to do with you?"

"I didn't give her the saddlebags."

"And, let's see. Madeline Dobbs has barely gotten out of bed in the past six days since her boyfriend of two years broke up with her, but you had no part in that."

"So I flirted a little. What can I say?"

"You cut off Katy Temple's hair at a cheerleader sleepover?"

"She should thank me. It was really damaged from her bad dye jobs."

"And Lucy Radzyminski is now enrolled at a private school because, her parents say, 'We couldn't stand to hear her cry anymore. We wanted her to be somewhere where she could make friends.'" Irirangi looked up from her notes. "Again, nothing to do with you?"

"Lucy's just not very likeable."

"That's unfortunate," said Irirangi. "And if you were in Lucy's situation, how would you deal with people not liking you?"

"I don't know. Never had that problem."

"Really? Everyone likes you?"

"Everyone who matters."

"You must be very special," Irirangi said.

"Oh, I am."

"So how does a special girl like you end up in my office on a Friday afternoon, labeled a bully by her principal?" asked Irirangi. "It seems to me that others see you differently than you see yourself. Why do you think that is?"

"Because they're stupid."

"Is everyone stupid except you?"

"Maybe."

"You mentioned a boyfriend a minute ago. Is he stupid?"

"Oh, completely. He's an idiot."

"And yet you're dating him?"

"He's an idiot who's also a senior with a Mercedes SLK fifty-five AMG and a lake house. And he makes nice arm candy."

"So is it idiotic that he cares about you? Maybe even loves you?"

"Tristan? Please!" Brinkley laughed. "I'm a trophy girlfriend. Our relationship is what you might call mutually beneficial."

"That doesn't sound terribly romantic, does it?"

"Can't we just skip to the part where you tell me I have an Electra complex or something gross like that? This is getting boring."

"All right, then," Irirangi said, "let's cut to the chase. Your boyfriend doesn't love you. Does anyone love Brinkley Harper?"

"Oh, here we go!" Brinkley said. "What's my line? My mother never loved me? Sorry. My mom adores me. So does my dad. You'd better get some other Freud or whatever up your sleeve, because I'm not going to give you anything you can use. I'm perfectly sane. A fine specimen of mental health."

"You want to know what I think?" Irirangi said.

"I can hardly wait."

"I think that you're afraid to be here because you think you might tell me something about yourself you don't want others to know."

"Such as?"

"I don't know. That's what we need to find out."

"Good save!" Brinkley exclaimed. "You're going to have to step up your game, Doc."

"Maybe you're right about that," said Irirangi. "I think we're finished for today. You said you had something for me to sign?"

Brinkley took a piece of paper out of her backpack. "I have to give this to the principal Monday morning to prove I showed up." She handed it to Irirangi, who signed it and gave it back. "You could just write on there that my therapy's complete and I don't have to come back. There's a space for comments."

"I wouldn't write comments," said Irirangi. "Our sessions are confidential."

"Go ahead. I give you permission. I've got nothing to hide."

Irirangi took the paper again from Brinkley. She wrote on it and gave it back.

"'Client appears to suffer from Narcissistic Personality Disorder'," Brinkley said. "'Further intensive therapy strongly recommended.' What's up with that?"

"Normally, I wouldn't diagnose a patient so early," said Irirangi. "And most practitioners frown on even telling narcissists what they are because they a) refuse to believe it and b) seldom change their behavior even when their disorder is pointed out to them. But since you seemed so eager to get things going. . . . I'll see you tomorrow."

"But tomorrow is Saturday! You can't expect me to come on weekends!"

"Very well. You can have Sunday off," said Irirangi.

"But I have plans!"

"So do I," the counselor said. "I have some very special therapy planned for you. See you tomorrow."

chapter two

Brinkley wore an old velour Juicy Couture track suit and no makeup to the Saturday session. Irirangi could make her show up, but she couldn't make her participate, and she certainly couldn't make her happy to be there.

"You like photographs?" Irirangi asked as she settled into her chair with an armful of pictures on black cardboard backings.

"If they're of me," Brinkley said. "That narcissistic enough for you?"

Irirangi ignored the comment. "I'm going to show you some photographs of some people you've never met. All teen girls, about your age. I want you to tell me what you think of each girl."

Irirangi flipped up the first board. The photo was of a beautiful blonde with flowing hair, full lips, blue eyes, and a tiny nose. It could almost have been a picture of Brinkley. "Loser," Brinkley said.

"What makes you say that?"

"Just look in her eyes. She's a total wannabe. And she's got on too many necklaces."

"She looks like the cover of a magazine to me," said Irirangi.

"To you, probably."

"All right. Let's look at another one."

Brinkley immediately said, "Yuck! Look at those shoes!"

"That's the first thing you noticed about this girl?" Irirangi said. "Her face is beautiful, her skin is flawless, her hair is shiny, she's perfectly proportioned—and the first thing you notice is her shoes?"

"Duh! Who could look away from those roadkill high-tops? She looks like Frankenstein in those things!"

"Moving along . . . ." Irirangi held up a vintage photograph of a young woman from the Depression era.

"Fashion victim."

Brinkley responded to dozens more photos with some sort of criticism: *lipstick's the wrong color; rabbit teeth; looks like a slut; goody two-shoes; somebody give her a comb; cankles; MoonPie face; my Aunt Susie called and she wants her Chadwicks of Boston outfit back.*

Three or four of the girls in the photographs were particularly thin, beautiful, well-dressed, and, in Brinkley's estimation, didn't appear to be "trying too hard." Of them, she said, "She could probably hang with me."

Last, Irirangi showed her a photograph of a teen girl with short spiky jet black hair, black eye makeup extending to her temples, two cheek piercings, a lip piercing, and purposely ripped black clothes. Brinkley recoiled. "Please! I just had breakfast!"

"What's wrong with this girl?"

"You're serious?"

"Have you ever considered that maybe you're placing too much emphasis on appearances?" Irirangi asked.

"Isn't it time to go yet?" said Brinkley. "How much longer do I have to look at pictures of ugly people? This sucks!"

"Our time is almost up," said Irirangi. "I appreciate your candor today."

Brinkley felt proud of herself for having kept her foot firmly planted on the bitch brake the entire session. She was sure she'd exhausted the counselor with her negativity. "Always glad to do my part," she said. "Can I go now?"

"Yes," said Irirangi. "Yes, Brinkley. You may go." She seemed to be thinking hard about something. "And Brinkley," she added, just as Brinkley opened the door to leave.

"What?"

"Sleep well."

"It's barely nine o'clock. You dragged me out of bed on a Saturday, and now you're telling me to sleep well?"

"Yes. Rest is very important for an adolescent. Through our rest, we are reborn to each new day."

"Is that something you saw burned into wood and shellacked at a folk-art festival?"

"Monday," said Irirangi. "Come by right after school."

chapter three

Monday morning, Brinkley was going about her usual routine of drying her hair when she suddenly stopped and stared at the mirror, horrified. On the left side of her face, where she brushed over the layer that hit just below her chin to bring attention to her perfectly shaped full lips, there was a dark black streak where there should have been pale highlights.

"Mom!" Brinkley called. "MOM!"

"What is it, Brinkley? I'm running late. I should've been there fifteen minutes ago."

"Look at my hair! Would you look at this?"

"Why did you put a black streak in your gorgeous blonde hair?" her mother asked.

"That's the thing—I didn't! How could my hair just turn black all of a sudden?"

"I don't know. It's probably some weird chemical reaction or something. Maybe some new product you're using interacted with the peroxide in the highlights?"

"But I haven't used any new products!"

"OK, sweetie, I'm sorry about your hair, but I have to run. Wear a hat or something."

Brinkley didn't have time to rewash her hair altogether, so she tried washing out the streak in the sink. No luck. Since her mom had been no help, Brinkley tried to find Tallulah, but the housekeeper had already left to go grocery shopping and wouldn't be back before Brinkley had to leave for school.

Brinkley determined that she had no choice but to work the black streak. She made a mental note, however, that her colorist's head would roll. Seventy-five-dollar touch-ups every three weeks and this was the thanks she got? Her mom must've been right: It was some sort of strange chemical reaction. Her natural color wasn't even black, but dark blonde.

Brinkley frequently modeled her fashion, hair, and makeup after movies her friends had never heard of. They had no idea that some days she channeled Grace Kelly in *Rear Window* or that she had spent hours in front of a mirror perfecting the stony, raised-eyebrow stare of an indignant Vivien Leigh in *Gone with the Wind*. The result—that Brinkley was more fabulous, interesting, and mysterious than any other girl in school—felt to her very much deserved. She'd earned it. She saw her cinema obsession as a sort of secret research. Brinkley loved almost any movie so long as it was at least twenty years old. Even the less brilliant ones could be beneficial to a student of fashion.

The look she decided on for today was a hybrid: From the neck up, she'd be the image of Ursula Andress in *What's New Pussycat?*; the outfit, however, would combine that sixties mod feel with a touch of eighties *Flashdance*. Brinkley applied smoky eye shadow and liner along with peachy pink blush and lip gloss. Then she selected a gray fitted tee with a wide neckline over a black cami, making sure the bottom of the camisole as well as the right strap were visible. She paired the top with a denim mini, black mid-calf leggings, two black necklaces, a silver bangle bracelet, and a silver ring worn on her right thumb. Black Chuck Taylors made it look effortless. She cocked her head to one side, put her hands in her shirt pockets, and tossed her hair over her left shoulder. Taking one last adoring look at herself, she half smiled, half snarled. Oh yeah, she could rock this look.

"What's up with the black streak?" Brinkley's BFF, Bette Caravallo, asked when she got to school.

"Just something I felt like trying this morning," Brinkley said. Bette might have been her best friend, but that didn't mean Brinkley had to tell her everything. Because what if she told Bette the truth, and Bette told some of the other cheerleaders? Then it would be all over school and the black streak would be a joke. This way, everyone would think she'd done it on purpose. Better to operate from a position of strength.

"I *love* it," Bette said. "You're so cutting edge!"

Brinkley had no doubt that by lunch, everyone who was anyone would be talking about her black streak, wondering how they could get one without it being obvious that they'd copied her.

"Come on," Brinkley said. "I have to drop off this costume Tallulah sewed for the play."

"What play?"

"Duh! The one I got the lead in. I told you about it last month."

"Oh, yeah," Bette said. "I forgot. How come you never go to rehearsals or anything?"

"I go to rehearsals," said Brinkley, "sometimes."

"Who are you playing again?"

"Some chick named Laura Wingspan," Brinkley replied.

"Is she hot?"

"Um, hello? Obviously!"

The very idea. How could Brinkley Harper ever *not* be hot?

chapter four

In Brinkley's mind, Emma Paulis did not add up. A mousy girl who refused to acknowledge the importance of a good blowout and a bit of lipstick, Emma had graciously accepted even insignificant roles in all the high school plays. During her last audition, she'd shared her hope of winning a scholarship to study theater at a small women's college in Missouri. Brinkley found it hard to believe that people went to women's colleges of their own free will. And what was there to do in Missouri? She'd been surprised when Emma had auditioned against her for the lead: Emma didn't really seem the type who ought to be up in front of people in the first place.

But naturally, Brinkley had gotten the lead. She would be Laura Wingfield in *The Glass Menagerie.* Emma was just lucky to be Brinkley's understudy.

Emma was backstage when Brinkley and Bette came in to drop off the costume. "Hey," she said. Neither of the girls replied. When Brinkley took the costume out of the bag and laid it on the piano, Emma said, "Oh, Brinkley! It's perfect! It's going to be such a beautiful play, and Laura is a great part."

"Well, don't get any ideas. I don't plan on breaking a leg or whatever."

Emma laughed good-naturedly. "'Break a leg' is like saying 'good luck' in theater," she said, "so in that sense, I hope you will break a leg." She smiled.

Brinkley looked at her. "Are you threatening me?"

Emma's eyes widened. "No, of course not!"

"If you're messing with me, I will see to it that you don't work on this play at all!"

"But I . . . I didn't . . ."

"Leave her alone." Miranda Morrison came up, carrying paints for the scenery.

"Excuse me?" said Brinkley. "Do you have something to say to me, you Goth freak?" Miranda looked away. "Yeah, that's what I thought. Loser."

Suddenly, Miranda stepped right in front of her. Her black spike choker necklace matched her rubber bracelets, fingernail polish, T-shirt, belt, jeans, and combat boots. She had piercings in her nose and lips. Brinkley was stunned and a bit frightened: Miranda had never made eye contact with her before.

"I said, leave her alone!" Miranda yelled. "In the first place, you're too stupid to realize that Emma was trying to be gracious. In the second place, you have no idea what a huge gesture that is on Emma's part since everybody knows she's the one who really deserves the role you got."

"What did you just say?" Brinkley asked.

"You heard me. You know the only reason you got that part is because your family gave a big donation to the capital campaign, and they named the new auditorium after your dead grandmother. You couldn't act your way out of a paper bag. You butchered the monologue during the audition, and you hardly ever bother showing up for rehearsals anyway, so stop pretending that you care about any of this. And stop giving Emma a hard time!"

Emma, Bette, and Brinkley stood in stunned silence. Before

Brinkley could collect herself enough to answer, Bette pulled her away. "Come on, Brinks, let's go." Then, to Miranda, Bette said, "Why don't you go cut yourself or whatever it is you people do?"

Bette linked her arm through Brinkley's as they walked down the hall.

"Did you hear what that freak said to me?"

"Blow it off," Bette said. "Who cares what she thinks?"

Brinkley's boyfriend appeared and began walking with them. "What's up, babe?" he said, resting his arm around her shoulders.

"Not now, Tristan," Brinkley said, shrugging his arm away.

"What's your problem?" he asked.

Even though he was technically good looking and considered the catch of the school, something about Tristan mildly repulsed Brinkley. Perhaps it was the proliferation of man-jewelry—bracelet, earring, and necklace—that struck her as contrived and effeminate. She thought he should at least lose the necklace. Or maybe the bracelet. Or both. Come to think of it, she wasn't too big on guys with earrings, either.

"Our girl has had a very taxing morning, Tristan," Bette explained. "Some Goth-nobody had the nerve to tell her she didn't deserve the part."

"What part?"

"You know, the part in the school play. Brinks is the lead."

"Excuse me." Carly Myers eased past the three of them, smiling at Brinkley as she did. When she was a few feet away, Tristan mooed loudly. Brinkley was too preoccupied to even giggle.

"So, did you do the thingy you had to do not to get expelled?" Bette said.

"Yeah, it's all taken care of."

Tristan smacked his gum. "What'd you have to do again, anyway?"

"Nothing—just some stupid community service," Brinkley lied. "Stocking a food pantry for poor people. Stuff like that. I may have to do a few more hours of it; I'm not sure yet."

"Whatever," said Bette. "They'll never break you!"

Brinkley and Bette were known to Story High students as "The Killer B's"—a term the guys used because the two were "killer hot," and the other girls used because Brinkley and Bette, should you get on their wrong side, could destroy you more efficiently than the Special Forces. For the girls—especially those who'd transferred out of Story High to get away from the relentless attacks—the B in Killer B's stood for a word that was neither Brinkley nor Bette. Brinkley had always been the mastermind, but Bette had studied diligently at her master's feet for the past three years.

"The nerve of that girl!" Brinkley said. "I never want to see that Goth freak again!"

"That's going to be kind of hard since she's in our next class," said Bette. "But maybe that's a good thing."

"Why?"

"Because . . . you can't let her know she rattled you. You need to put her back in her place, and the sooner the better."

Brinkley thought a moment. "You're right, Bette. I need to remind her who's in charge around here."

chapter five

"I celebrate myself, and sing myself," Mrs. Nelson recited in first-period English. "'And what I assume you shall assume, / For every atom belonging to me as good belongs to you. / I loafe and invite my soul, / I lean and loafe at my ease observing a spear of summer grass.'"

LAME, Brinkley texted Bette as they sat in the back of the room.

"So, class," Mrs. Nelson continued, "any thoughts on Whitman's work so far?"

DUDE HAD WAY 2 MUCH FREE TIME, Bette texted back. Brinkley snickered.

"Brinkley?" Mrs. Nelson asked. "Perhaps you have something to share with the class?"

"Not really," Brinkley said with mock enthusiasm, "but thanks for the opportunity." The class giggled.

"But you seem so amused by Whitman's work. Do enlighten the rest of us, please."

Oh, you really don't want a piece of this, Brinkley thought. "I was just curious as to what type of grass Whitman was so into." The class laughed outright. "I mean, he needs to get a life already, if you ask me."

"Miranda," Mrs. Nelson said. "What do you think Whitman's message is?"

Brinkley rolled her eyes at Bette.

Miranda picked at the seam of her jeans and mumbled, "It's a statement about the oneness of all living things, the interconnectedness of the universe."

Mrs. Nelson sighed. "Thank you, Miranda. It's a relief that someone has some worthwhile insights to share."

KISS-UP, MUCH? Brinkley texted. 4 REAL, Bette replied. Brinkley nodded and removed her gum, sticking it under her desk.

After the bell rang and Mrs. Nelson had stepped out of the classroom, Brinkley and Bette stood in front of Miranda as she tried to leave. "Just so you know, freakbag, if you ever talk to me again like you did this morning, you will live to regret it."

"Look, I don't want any trouble." Miranda tried to walk around them.

"She's not so big and bad now," Bette said.

Miranda turned. "I think we all know that I could squash the two of you like the festering carbuncles you are. But I choose not to engage in petty behavior."

"What the hell's a carbuncle?" Bette said.

"I really don't think you want to start this." Miranda narrowed the distance between them. "You think you can intimidate me the way you did those other girls? You think I'll run away if you exclude me from the Story High social scene? Go ahead. Please. Give me a reason to show you just how much I care."

Brinkley and Bette stepped back.

"I'm not scared, if that's what you think," said Brinkley as Miranda brushed past. "You mouth off to me again, you'll be sorry!"

After Miranda left the room, Brinkley shivered. She never wanted to get that close to her again.

chapter six

ourth-period physics was a relief to Brinkley, not only today, but any day. The subject interested her little and her dad had bribed her with a Tod's handbag to take the course, but it was a break to have at least one period without anyone important watching her. With no one there to impress, she could relax and take time off from being the most popular girl in school, which was a great deal more taxing than the average person realized.

"What's up, homegirl?" asked Brinkley's lab partner, Matt Baker.

"Um, homegirl?" Brinkley said.

"Aw, now, don't be hatin' on a playa!" Matt said, pulling his jeans far down on his waist and striking a rapper pose. "Word to your mother!"

Brinkley couldn't help but laugh. "You are such a spaz!"

"Did you do your homework?" Matt asked.

"My dad told me I had to *take* physics, not pass it."

"Come on, Brinkley," Matt said, "you're missing out. Physics is awesome! In fact, science in general is just about the coolest thing there is."

"Don't oversell the nerd chic, Matt."

"No, I'm serious. Everything—every little daily phenomenon—has something to do with science. You can understand the universe! And what you can't understand yet, you can seek to understand through science."

"Matt, we've got to get you out more. Like, immediately." Matt grabbed the Coke can Brinkley was hiding behind the lab table. "Dude, you're going to get me busted!" she said. "Don't let Ms. Ouderkirk see that."

Matt began violently shaking the can.

"What are you doing?" Brinkley asked, reaching for the can just as Matt pulled it away from her.

"Showing you something cool," he said.

"Are you crazy? Now I can't even open it for like an hour or it will fizz everywhere."

"Give me twenty seconds," he said. He began tapping on the sides, top, and bottom of the can. When the twenty seconds had passed, he began pulling the tab.

"Matt, no!"

But when Matt opened the can, nothing came out but a little puff of vapor.

"How did you do that?"

Matt smiled. "Science, my dear!" he said. "When I shook the can, the gas mixed with the liquid and created pressure, but when I tapped the can's surface, I separated the gas from the liquid again. Thus, no fizz."

"Or, you could've just not shaken it at all, and there would still be no fizz."

"Come on! Admit that's pretty awesome!"

"I will admit this: I'm glad you're my lab partner because otherwise, I'd *so* be flunking this class."

"So then I can count on you to show up Saturday for the Physics Club doughnut sale? Bright and early, seven AM?"

"Yeah, right," Brinkley said.

"That reminds me—I'd better put something on the board about that. Physics Club president is a rewarding but thankless job." Matt went up to the board and wrote: DON'T FORGET—DOGNUT SALE THIS SATURDAY—7 AM

"You misspelled *doughnut*," Brinkley said when Matt returned to their lab table.

Matt said, "I know."

The lab work that day was on light refraction. Matt and Brinkley and the other teams had fifteen questions to answer and a small handheld laser to use for the experiment.

"These lasers suck," Matt said. "I think they bought them in like, 1988." He pointed the laser at Brinkley's forehead. "I'm melting your brain!" he said in an evil-scientist voice.

"Quit it!" Brinkley grabbed the laser out of Matt's hands.

"Relax—this thing is about as deadly as a flashlight," said Matt. "Our equipment is ancient. Now you see why I have to get up at seven AM on a Saturday to peddle the nuts of unsuspecting dogs."

"Excuse me? What the meaning is of this word?" It was that foreign exchange student—what was her name? Brinkley couldn't remember.

"Significant figures," Matt said. "Round up." He made a circular, upward hand motion.

"Thank you very much," she said.

"Why don't they learn English before they come over here?" Brinkley asked when the girl walked away.

"Brinkley, Jae Song is brilliant," Matt said. "Her English is fantastic considering she's only been here since fall semester. And she's head and shoulders above anybody in this class—including me—when it comes to math skills."

"So? She should still speak English."

Ginger Rue

"And how much Korean do you speak?"

"Yeah, well, I'm not in Korea, now, am I?"

"You're hopeless," Matt said. "You know, there's a whole world of people out there, Brinkley, and not all of them drive fancy cars or attend keg parties at your boyfriend's lake house."

"You don't have to get all testy," Brinkley said.

Matt laughed.

"What?" Brinkley asked. "Tell me you're not laughing because I said *testy*."

"Technically, the term is *testes*."

Matt kept on laughing, and Brinkley shoved him with her elbow.

She sort of liked having a dork for a friend. Not that she would admit that to any of her real friends, of course.

28

chapter seven

*B*rinkley surprised everyone when she showed up to rehearsal after school that day. Part of it was to prove Miranda wrong. The other part was to get out of her after-school counseling appointment. Irirangi's answering service had taken the call, so Brinkley didn't have to deal with her directly. She told them she'd call back to reschedule. Like that was going to happen.

By the time they got to scene two, Brinkley had already lost interest. "Laura?" Mr. Ellis said, "when the scene opens, you're polishing your collection of glass animals." Brinkley was absentmindedly staring up at the lights. "Brinkley," he said, "you're Laura. Remember?"

"Oh, OK, right." She found her place in the script and quickly read over it. "Hey, by the way, I wanted to talk to you about the costumes. I had my housekeeper sew mine based on the pattern you gave me, and she got the fabric you told her to, but all these clothes, they're totally hideous."

"The costuming isn't supposed to be red-carpet, Brinkley," Mr. Ellis replied. "The clothes the characters wear tell us a lot about them—their family, their personalities, their economic station and aspirations."

"Uh-huh, so I was thinking, maybe for Laura, I have this really cute BCBG Max Azria dress and some high-heeled boots—"

"Brinkley! No!" Mr. Ellis said. "That's completely inappropriate for the character! Laura Wingfield doesn't polish her glass collection while dressed like a fashion model!"

"Oh, yeah . . . about that . . . why *is* Laura always polishing glass? Nobody does that."

"Brinkley, dear," Mr. Ellis said, "the title of the play is *The Glass Menagerie.* It's kind of important to the story. You have read the script all the way through, haven't you?"

"Not exactly," Brinkley said, scanning the page. "But whatever. Let's roll with it." She read from the script: "How was your dahr meeting?"

"D, A, R," Mr. Ellis said. "The letters. Daughters of the American Revolution."

Brinkley shrugged. "All right." The actors continued with the scene but a few lines later, Mr. Ellis interrupted again.

"Brinkley, I don't think you're getting the spirit of your character. Laura is a fragile, frightened little thing. You're reading the lines with too much sassiness. Try again, please, from that last line you just read."

"'Please don't stare at me, Mother!'" Brinkley said, sounding like a reality show diva.

"You know what?" Mr. Ellis said. "Let's call it a day, and everyone try to read through the entire script before tomorrow's practice, all right?"

❀

Cocoa barked and squealed when Brinkley came in that afternoon. No matter what Brinkley's day at school had been like, Cocoa was always glad to see her. She scooped him up in her arms and kissed him as he shook all over with excitement.

"Miss Brinkley, I've prepared your dinner," said Tallulah. It was just past six o'clock. Brinkley had required a little shopping after rehearsal to calm her nerves. The incident with Miranda still had her somewhat shaken. "Shall I warm it for you?"

Brinkley asked, "What is it?"

"Grilled salmon," said Tallulah.

"You didn't put any of those disgusting capers on it this time, did you?"

"No. I remembered. It's just the way you like it."

"Put it in the fridge. I might warm it up later."

"Very well. Oh, and Dr. Harper called. She said she would be late tonight. Mr. Harper will also be late."

"What else is new?" Brinkley said.

"I ironed all your laundry and hung it in your closet," said Tallulah. "Will you require anything else?"

"No," said Brinkley. "You can go."

Tallulah looked at Brinkley with concern and said, "You're sure you're all right alone in the main house, Miss Brinkley? Your parents probably won't be home before you go to bed."

"I know the drill," she replied. "I'll buzz your apartment if I need you, and to keep me company, I have Cocoa." Cocoa nuzzled her cheek.

When Tallulah retired for the evening, Brinkley put away her new purchases, watched some television, and surfed the Web awhile. She'd gotten a group invitation on Facebook. She clicked it. It was from Matt Baker:

Matt Baker has invited you to join the Facebook group WOMEN IN LOVE WITH MATT BAKER. Accept? Decline? Ignore?

Brinkley couldn't resist. She clicked *accept*.

Not surprisingly, Matt was the admin, and it was an open group that anyone could join. So far, he had fifty-seven members, mostly people she didn't recognize, and many of them middle-aged women. The description said, *"Welcome to WOMEN IN LOVE WITH MATT BAKER. It was getting difficult to keep up with the growing number, hence the need for an official group. Sure, most of the members are friends of my mom's, but don't let that stop you from declaring your wanton desires. Don't forget to tell your friends. Matt's got love for everybody."*

Brinkley typed a comment. "Matt, U sexy beast! UR such a goober!!!"

Brinkley decided to call it a night since no one else had any exciting posts. (Did she really need to know that someone had taken the Which-*Grease*-Character-Are-You? quiz and that someone else was bored?) She felt exceedingly tired and looked forward to the prospect of her warm bed. "I hope I'm not getting sick," she said to herself. She set her cell to wake her up a bit later than usual and crawled into bed with Cocoa.

What was it that Irirangi had said about the importance of sleep to adolescents? Maybe there was something to that. Before long, the softness of nine hundred–thread–count sheets and the warmth of her fluffy comforter slipped her out of her day's concerns.

⸙

When Brinkley awoke, Cocoa wasn't there. *Maybe I've overslept,* she thought, *and Tallulah has already come and let him out.* Brinkley noticed that the surface under her head was hard and cold, and the sound rousing her from sleep wasn't her cell alarm. It was . . . giggling?

She opened one eye and saw a face she'd seen before but couldn't place. It was some guy . . . some nobody . . . from school. What was he doing in her house? Immediately, she sat up, ready to demand that he get out of her room. But when she looked around, she wasn't in her room.

She was in a classroom at Story.

"Miranda, did you get your beauty sleep?" the teacher asked. The class giggled again. Brinkley stared, mouth open. Why was the teacher looking at *her?*

This is weird, she thought. She shifted in the desk to get up and walk out of the room, but when she looked down at her legs, she didn't recognize them.

She was wearing black combat boots: beaten up, heavily worn black combat boots. To check if they were real, she touched one, but it wasn't her hand touching it. The fingers were shorter, and the nails were coated in black polish.

She looked at the rest of her body. She was wearing dark gray jeans with extra rivets, a riveted black belt, a black tee with dark purple letters that said DISTURB THE BALANCE, and black rubber bracelets. She put her hands to her throat and felt a dog-collar-style necklace. She didn't even recognize her own lithe, perfect figure: this one was shorter, the hips were wide-ish, the arms somewhat meatier and stumpy . . . and from the extra cushioning she felt against the chair, she inferred that she must have more butt than she was accustomed to.

Brinkley dashed for the door.

"Where are you going?" the teacher asked.

Brinkley could feel adrenaline running through her. "Bathroom," she replied as she ran out.

In the bathroom, Brinkley rushed to the mirror. Yesterday's black streak was still there. In fact, her hair was entirely black.

And the face looking back at her was not her own.

It was Miranda Morrison's.

chapter eight

What kind of weird dream was this? Brinkley needed to wake up, and fast.

She pinched herself, noting the extra flesh. Ick. Miranda was probably a size eight, and Brinkley, though she was tall, had never worn anything larger than a two. Brinkley splashed cold water on her face. If this was a dream, she wasn't waking up.

Brinkley hid out in a stall for a while. She heard the bell ring for the next class and students coming and going as though everything were normal. About ten minutes after the tardy bell had rung, Brinkley decided she was afraid to be alone, so she wandered into the hallway. The only other person in the hall was one of the coaches, and he looked just as normal as ever, which was not necessarily good news for him but was strangely comforting to Brinkley. She was just about to ask him for help when he said, "Miranda, get to class."

"That's just the thing," Brinkley said. "See . . . I'm *not* Miranda."

"Uh-huh," the coach said. "Listen, you Goth kids all look alike to me, but I know who you are." He called the office on his walkie-talkie and asked where Miranda Morrison was supposed to be that period. Then he escorted her to a classroom.

"Well?" the teacher said. "Take your seat."

Brinkley looked around the room. Since she wasn't in this class, she had no idea where Miranda sat. There were plenty of people she knew, but none of them even looked up at her. "Over here?" she asked, pointing toward an empty desk. The teacher nodded, looking confused.

The class was working silently on some sort of assignment, but Brinkley, having neither a backpack nor even a notebook, sat and stared.

"Miranda, where are your materials?" the teacher asked.

"I . . . I don't know," Brinkley replied.

"You, coming to class unprepared? That isn't like you," the teacher said, writing a hall pass.

"Tell me about it," said Brinkley.

"Go get your things."

But where *were* Miranda's things? Her locker? And where was that?

She went to the office. "May I help you?" asked Mrs. Ingram, the secretary.

"Do you know where Mir . . . *my* locker is?"

"It's the second semester of school, and you don't know where your locker is?"

"Well, of course I know where my locker is," Brinkley said, laughing nervously. "It's just that I . . . I forgot."

"You *forgot.*" Mrs. Ingram sighed and pulled a little gray box out of a locked desk drawer. "Name?"

"Morrison."

"Locker number one forty-nine."

"Thanks. And what's the combination?"

Mrs. Ingram leaned over the counter and whispered conspiratorially, "Are you on something?"

"I'm not sure," Brinkley said.

"Very funny. Four, twenty-two, thirty-two."

Brinkley went to Miranda's locker and grabbed a notebook. It was covered in band names Brinkley had never heard of. As Brinkley was examining the notebook's cover, the bell rang. She'd taken so much time going to the office that the class she'd gone to get the notebook for was over. A Goth boy passing by tapped one of the strange symbols on her notebook. "DK—rock on!" he said.

"Donna Karan?" she replied.

The boy laughed. "Good one. I love the Dead Kennedys—kickin' it old school!" He stuck out his tongue and made a hand sign with his index and pinky fingers extended and his middle fingers held down by his thumb. Unsure how to respond, Brinkley returned the hand gesture and also stuck out her tongue. Was that a—it was! Ewww! "There's a hole in my tongue!" she said to no one in particular.

Then someone put a hand on her shoulder. "Don't forget our appointment this period," said Mrs. Jacobs, a school counselor.

"Appointment?"

"I know. Hard to believe it's been another month already. I'm just going to grab a cup of coffee in the teacher's lounge, and then I'll be right there. See you in a sec."

Great, Brinkley thought. *Just what I need—another stupid counselor.*

chapter nine

$\mathcal{W}$hatever was going on, there was no way Brinkley was going to continue walking around dressed like a sideshow freak. She went to her own locker and retrieved a makeup bag and an oversized pink jacket. In the restroom, she took off the spiked choker, washed off Miranda's black makeup, and applied some pastels instead. With the pink jacket on, Miranda almost looked normal. Except for that horrible jet black hair, but there was only so much Brinkley could do.

As she sat in the counselor's office, Brinkley tried to get her head around what was happening. If she wasn't dreaming, what was going on? If she was Miranda, where was Brinkley? And was Miranda still Miranda, somewhere else, at the same time? And if so, where was she? And did Miranda know this was happening? What if Miranda had turned into *her*? And if so, what would Miranda *do* to her?

"How's your progress?" Mrs. Jacobs asked.

"Fine?" Brinkley offered.

The counselor stared at her. "Just fine? I mean, how many times since our last session?"

How many times what?

"May I see?" Mrs. Jacobs grabbed the cuff of Miranda's oversized boot-cut jeans and pulled it up. The jeans were baggy and didn't hug the calves the way Brinkley's did, so the counselor easily pulled them

over the knee. There, on the lower thigh, Brinkley saw the scars—
two to three inches each in length. She let out a small gasp.

"Are you all right?"

"I'm fine."

"I wouldn't say entirely fine. That one's new," said Mrs. Jacobs,
pointing to one of the marks on Miranda's leg. "What was the trigger?"

"Trigger?"

"Come on, Miranda. What happened?"

"I . . . I don't know."

"Miranda, these cuts don't happen by themselves. Something
triggered you. Have you been practicing the positive self-talk?"

"Yes?"

"Was it your stepdad again?"

"My stepdad?"

"Let's say it together: My stepdad is a . . . what, Miranda?"

Brinkley had no idea what to say. How was she supposed to know
what Miranda's stepdad was?

"Miranda? Let me hear you say it: My stepdad is a . . . ?"

"Construction worker?"

"Miranda."

"Dental hygienist?"

"Stop using humor to hide from this. You know what your stepdad is. Say it for me: my stepdad is a domestic terrorist."

"My stepdad is a domestic terrorist?" What did that even mean?
Did he, like, blow up federal buildings?

"It's all right to label him what he is. Don't be afraid. It's healthier
to acknowledge abusive behavior than to try to make excuses for it
or pretend it's OK. And if you let him get inside your head, you're
letting him control you. But who controls Miranda Morrison?"

Brinkley found the question interesting, given the situation. "Miranda Morrison?"

"Yes. You control your reactions, even to other people's bad behavior. You can't change your stepfather, but you can control how you respond to him. How about at school, with your peers? How's that going?"

"Fine."

"I heard you had a run-in with Brinkley Harper."

"Who told you that?"

"That's not important. But I was pleasantly surprised to hear that you felt confident enough to stand up to that crowd. That's a big step for you."

"Look, Brinkley's not so bad," she said.

"Miranda, like I was saying about your stepdad, it's healthy to label inappropriate behavior for what it is and not to make excuses for it. Brinkley Harper has driven at least four girls away from this school with her campaign of torment, and I'm glad to hear you're standing up for yourself. That's a positive, healthy thing to do. We cannot change Brinkley Harper, but we can change how we respond to her. We can refuse to let her hurt you."

"It's not Brinkley's fault I'm a freak," Brinkley said.

"Hold on a minute, there. No matter what Brinkley Harper says, I want you to remember that being different doesn't make you a freak. You have to work on your ability to reframe. Different can mean special, too. The great musicians, artists, all of them might have been called freaks as well, because they were different. But what if they hadn't been different? What if they'd been just like everyone else? What would hang in the Louvre?"

Brinkley smirked.

"What?" Mrs. Jacobs asked.

"Maybe I'll be like Van Gogh and cut off my ear and give it to you," she said.

Mrs. Jacobs recoiled. "Why would you say such a thing, Miranda?"

"I thought it was pretty funny."

"I don't understand your attitude today," Mrs. Jacobs said. "I'm troubled by your glib comments and the way you seem to be identifying with your oppressors."

"Can I go now?"

"One more thing," she said. "What made you want to try this new makeup and the pink jacket?"

"I don't know."

"Don't be self-conscious," Mrs. Jacobs said. "I think this is a healthy sign. It shows you're trying something new. A bit of a break, perhaps, from the tough exterior you've worked so hard to cultivate."

"I gotta go," Brinkley said.

The next period was lunch. Brinkley hoped Miranda had some money in her account, even though it was spongy-chicken-nuggets day. She was positively starving. She went through the line and got her tray. Then she looked around the lunchroom. Where did people like Miranda sit, anyway?

A smattering of black over in one corner caught her eye. Yeah, that must be the place. She passed the table where her crowd sat. She was relieved not to see herself sitting there. Tristan was sitting next to Bette. Brinkley heard him say, "Where is she, anyway?" Naturally, everyone was wondering where she was. She'd have to tell them she'd been out sick when she turned back into herself . . . *if* she turned back into herself. *Don't worry about that right now,* Brinkley thought. *One thing at a time.*

Brinkley made her way to the corner and sat down with the other freaks. She was so hungry, she began eating without saying a word to anyone. That was probably what Goths did anyway. There were only a handful of them in the entire school, and since they disdained everyone else, they probably disdained each other, too.

"You going Barbie doll on us or something?" one of the girls asked.

"I beg your pardon?" Brinkley said.

"What's up with the pink jacket? And your makeup is, like, all Malibu Barbie."

"I know, Miranda!" said one of the guys. "You got L'Oréal . . . because you're worth it!"

"Get bent," Brinkley said.

"Hey, you're the one trying to look like *them,*" he said, gesturing to the masses.

Brinkley was in no mood.

"Oh, right. So let me get the rules straight," she replied. "In order to not conform, I have to look different from them. But this nonconformity requires conforming to look like you. Is that it? Is that how you bring on the big Goth revolution? By making sure that you all conform to the nonconformity?"

"You don't have to be a total bitch about it," the guy said.

"Back off, dude. She's right," said the girl who'd originally asked about her makeup. What was her name? "Miranda keeps it real."

Brinkley felt a strange gratitude to the girl for sticking up for her . . . or . . . for Miranda. "Thank you . . ." Brinkley struggled to remember the girl's name but came up empty. "Thank you, O Princess of Darkness." That was probably a compliment to these freaks, right?

The girl giggled. "Just call me POD!"

The guy who'd been smacked down said to POD, "I was just ragging on her a little bit. Come on, you two. Lighten up."

Brinkley couldn't help but laugh. A Goth had told her to lighten up. Priceless.

"So?"

"So what?" Brinkley replied.

"So let's see it."

"See what?"

POD sighed and moved Miranda's hair off her ear. "Sweet!" she said.

Brinkley lifted her hand and felt an inch-long steel rod impaling the upper cartilage of her right ear. Wasn't the hole in her tongue enough? What was Miranda trying to become, a human pin cushion? "Son of a—"

"Nice!" the guy who'd teased her about her hair interrupted.

Brinkley was torn between two conflicting impulses: The first, to keep her hand covering the wounded, violated ear; the second, to pull her hand away for fear of touching it. "Do you have a mirror?" she asked POD.

"What do I look like, Brinkley Harper?"

"You wish," Brinkley mumbled.

"What?"

"Nothing." Brinkley picked up a spoon and tried to use the backside of it as a mirror, but it was no use. All she could see was a blurred reflection of Miranda's face. "I have a *pole* rammed through my *ear*," she said to the other people at the table. "And this is something I did to myself on *purpose?*"

They all nodded, confused by the question.

"Just to clarify," Brinkley continued. "This isn't some horrible freak accident where I somehow get a *pole* rammed through my *ear,* and go immediately to the emergency room to have the *pole* removed *from* my *ear?* As in, taken completely *out* because it's a foreign object that in no way, shape, or form *belongs* there?"

"What's the matter with you, Miranda?" asked POD. "Why all the verbal italics? You look badass. Listen, are you hanging with us tonight? Or were you planning on some family fun at home with your mom and Daddy Dearest?"

"Duh!" said another girl. "It's Tuesday. She's gotta work."

Oh, crap, Brinkley thought. *In addition to several superfluous and in no way attractive piercings, Miranda has a job.*

chapter ten

$\mathcal{J}$ ust because Miranda had a job didn't mean that Brinkley was going to do it for her. That was Miranda's problem, after all, not hers. Though she desperately wanted to go home, she knew she couldn't just walk into her own house this way. Tallulah would call the cops or have a heart attack before she could even pick up the phone. Brinkley knew her parents wouldn't be home yet, and if they were, what would she say to them? They wouldn't believe she was stuck in someone else's body. She'd just have to go to Miranda's house and hang out until this nightmare or hallucination or whatever it was subsided.

Of course, she had to figure out how to get to Miranda Morrison's house, wherever that was.

There was what appeared to be a house key in Miranda's locker, but no car keys. Apparently, Miranda had no car, a prospect that dismayed Brinkley. It was like hearing that someone didn't have food or that their house had only one bathroom. Luckily, the Goth who had earlier teased her about her makeup offered her a ride and dropped her off in front of an average-looking lower-middle-class house. The front door was unlocked. She slipped inside the dark and dank-smelling living room. The blinds and curtains were closed. There were no plants or any knickknacks to give the place atmosphere.

A woman rushed over in stockinged feet and quietly closed the door behind Brinkley. She put a finger to her lips and pulled Brinkley past an old plaid couch, where a scruffy, unshaven man in a flannel shirt lay sleeping with several empty beer bottles scattered around him. His mouth was open, and he snored lightly.

When they got to the hallway, the woman—she must have been Miranda's mother—said, "Are you crazy? Why didn't you come in the back? You know how he gets if you wake him."

Brinkley wondered just how exactly he did get, but wasn't sure she really wanted to know. "I'm sorry," she said.

Miranda's mother smiled. "Hey, what can I get for you? Do you want a sandwich before work? You don't have much time. Better get dressed, honey. If we're lucky, he'll sleep until after you're gone."

On second thought, Brinkley decided, *maybe I will go to Miranda's job.*

Brinkley declined the sandwich. There were only two bedrooms and one bathroom, so Miranda's bedroom wasn't hard to find. The other room had a pair of men's boots by the bed, so she assumed that one belonged to Miranda's parents. But except for the lack of men's shoes, there was nothing about Miranda's room that suggested a teenage girl's room, either. It had plain beige walls and a bed with no headboard. There were no bulletin boards with diagonal pink ribbons and buttons holding photos of smiling girls on a beach trip or at an amusement park. The room's only distinctive characteristic was a corner table covered with all sorts of candles, most of which were well used and had hardened wax drippings along the sides. The table had a couple of campy miniatures of the Virgin Mary and a crucifix, as though the area were some sort of shrine.

Miranda's mother had told her to get dressed for work, so Brinkley quietly closed the door behind her and looked in the closet. Nothing but black clothes, except for a couple of green polo shirts with the words IRELAND'S KITCHEN embroidered in orange. Brinkley's stomach did a little flip. Of all the cheesy places . . .

The door handle turned slowly, and Miranda's mother poked her head in. Then she slipped inside and shut the door behind her, careful to turn the knob and release it so that there was no noise. "If we leave in the next few minutes," she said, "I can drive you to work and he'll never know we were here. You get dressed, and I'll meet you outside."

The sensation Brinkley felt in her stomach from seeing the Ireland's shirt was nothing compared to the tight coil she felt now. When she closed the closet door and the hinges squeaked, she actually shushed them.

During the car ride with Miranda's mom, Brinkley didn't say a word. She was too busy worrying that she might never change back to herself. What if she stayed in Miranda's body forever? That would be worse than a death sentence. Though she'd never given a thought to Miranda's life before, it was worse than anything she might have imagined, living in fear of that man on the couch. The school counselor had called him a "domestic terrorist," hadn't she? What, exactly, did that mean? Yet Brinkley kept silent as Miranda's mother fiddled with the radio and made small talk. She didn't want to ask questions about Miranda's dad. Miranda's mother asked her about school, smiled more than necessary, and chattered on about the people she worked with.

"Well, here we are," said Miranda's mom.

What was Brinkley supposed to do now? She'd never worked in a restaurant—or anywhere—before. She'd never even *eaten* in a dump like this.

"Thanks for the ride," Brinkley said. "Um . . . any idea how long I have to be here?"

"Your shift is until nine tonight, isn't it?"

"Right. Nine. So, I guess I'll see you when you pick me up?"

"Sweetie, are you all right? You know I'm working till midnight at the hospital. Can't you catch a ride?"

"Oh . . . oh, yeah," Brinkley said. "What was I thinking? Of course I'll catch a ride. That's what I always do because I'm Miranda Morrison and you're my mom and this is where I work apparently every Tuesday, and probably some other days, too."

Miranda's mom smiled weakly. "Thanks, honey. Have a good night. I love you."

Since she'd been dropped off by the back door, Brinkley went inside through a storage room of some sort. There was a big punch-card machine and some alphabetized cards. She'd seen one of these contraptions in a movie once. She pulled Miranda's card out of its slot and fed it to the clock machine. It made a loud punching noise, then released the card, and Brinkley put it back in Miranda's slot. She pushed open the kitchen door and was immediately confronted by a sign that read, EMPLOYEES MUST WASH HANDS BEFORE ENTERING KITCHEN.

Brinkley had barely gotten her hands washed when a man with a mustache that looked like it had time-traveled from 1973 yelled, "This order is ready, Morrison!"

"I just got here," she said.

"It's called teamwork, Morrison! Look it up!"

Brinkley grabbed the plates and put them on the tray the manager had shoved at her. "Table twelve!" he barked.

Brinkley walked through a pair of swinging doors into a little station where other servers were pouring coffee and tea. She stood staring at them. When a waiter looked at her, Brinkley said, "I just got here," not knowing what else to say.

"I'll tell the hostess," the boy said.

"Thanks," said Brinkley, unsure of what that meant. "Where's table twelve?"

"You're not really going to serve those, are you?"

"I have to. . . . That man yelled at me to do it."

The boy raised his eyebrows and offered a sarcastic, "Good luck."

"Which one is table twelve?" asked Brinkley.

The boy pointed it out to her. "How can you not know where table twelve is? You've worked here longer than I have."

"I'm altered," Brinkley replied. Surely, people would believe Miranda was on drugs. And it was a good cover.

Brinkley delivered the dishes to table twelve. Then she went back to the area just outside the kitchen to find out what to do next. A woman in her late thirties, hardened and bitter-looking, was yelling at a cowering teenage girl. "Did you serve my table?" she demanded. "'Cause you know what I've told you about serving my tables!"

"Kristen, it wasn't me!" the girl insisted.

The woman began shouting over the heads of the scurrying wait-staff. "Nobody serves my tables, everybody got that? It cuts into my tips. The customers think I'm slacking. You serve my tables, you can expect to get your ass kicked. Understand?"

Brinkley thought about the day before when Miranda had frightened her. She took a few steps into the angry waitress's personal space, looked the woman dead in the eye, and said stonily, "I served table twelve."

Kristen's eyes grew slightly bigger, and her mouth opened for just a split second before she recovered herself. "Oh, well," she said, "all right then. Rodriguez make you?"

"I got the 'teamwork-look-it-up' bit," Brinkley said without an ounce of humor.

Kristen laughed nervously. "Yeah, I hate that one. Oh, look . . . we're almost out of biscuits. I'll get some."

Brinkley smiled as she mimicked the activity of another waiter who'd also just clocked in, counting out sets of silverware rolled in green cloth napkins. Kristen was scared of her—and not because she might say something about her to the cheerleaders at the lunch table. It felt sort of, well . . . marvelous. Maybe there was something to all this black hair and black clothes. They seemed to bring a certain level of respect, didn't they? Or at least a handy "back off!" vibe.

Once the helpful waiter boy had shown her which tables were her responsibility (and suggested she lay off the drugs), Brinkley quickly picked up the routine of taking orders, sending them to the kitchen, and bringing out plates of food. In between, she refilled glasses with water or sodas. She was yelled at a total of three times by Rodriguez: twice for not writing the orders down according to the standard kitchen lingo—CHIX instead of CHICKEN, for example—and once for failing to "marry the sauces."

"You're supposed to marry the sauces at your tables as soon as you clock in!" Rodriguez said.

Brinkley looked at him as though he'd lost his mind. "I beg your pardon?" The helpful waiter boy stood behind Rodriguez with two ketchup bottles and mimed pouring the sauce from one into the other while Rodriguez continued his rant. "Customers should never have a half-empty bottle of ketchup! You know that. Sloppy, Morrison, sloppy!"

Brinkley'd had enough of this guy.

"First of all, as soon as I clocked in, you made me serve someone else's table," she said. "Second of all, maybe my sauces didn't want to get married. Maybe they're too young. Maybe they just want to live together for a while and see how things go. And third, maybe I'm having a bad night but I'm working my butt off—so can you just let me do my job without hounding me?"

She realized Rodriguez might fire her. But it wasn't Brinkley's stupid job anyway, right? He'd be doing Brinkley a favor.

"Get to work, Morrison," Rodriguez said. Then he turned and walked back into the kitchen. Either Rodriguez, too, was afraid of Miranda, or it was too hard to get people to take this crappy job, and he didn't want to fire someone who'd already been trained. Whatever it was, he left her alone.

The five-hour shift was the most physically grueling thing Brinkley had ever done. Not only did she have to serve the customers, she also had to clean up after each table, and most of them didn't seem to mind leaving errant biscuit crumbs all over the place for her to pick up with her floor sweeper. Not to mention the fact that, while she was tired and starving, she had to serve hot, buttery food to other people without stopping for so much as a snack. And she had to deal with those annoying kids-eat-free-with-each-adult-dinner coupons. The parents seemed to find it adorable when their kids threw food at her or spilled their drinks all over the place.

And then there was the birthday singing.

"I've got a live one," a waiter would announce in the preparation area. "Who's going to sing the stupid song with me?" Everyone would groan. "Come on—don't make me get Rodriguez after you. Somebody's gotta do it." Four or five other members of the waitstaff would accompany him to the table and sing the Ireland's Kitchen birthday song:

We hear it is your birthday, lad (lass)—
We know that you've been wishin'
To come and claim your pot o'gold
Here at Ireland's Kitchen!

The staff was expected to sing with heart and dance an Irish jig, kicking up their heels and linking arms with the birthday schmuck, who was then presented with a plastic cauldron containing a cake smothered in gold icing. The staff also gave him a necklace of shiny green beads with a plastic medallion that said, I CAUGHT THE BIRTHDAY LEPRECHAUN AT IRELAND'S KITCHEN!

There were three birthdays that night, and Brinkley sang and danced the jig for each one of them. Whenever someone would ask for singers, she would groan and comment about how she loathed having no choice in the matter.

But no matter how busy she was, she never ducked out.

For the two minutes or so it took to complete the song and routine, she would kick, stomp, and sway with abandon, chanting the goofy tune spiritedly . . .

. . . forgetting all about the man on the couch, the stark room with the candles, and what it was like to be Miranda Morrison. It was the one instance in which she could step out of the character of the gloomy Goth girl, and Brinkley welcomed the respite. She wondered if Miranda did, too. *She must,* Brinkley thought. *I know she does.*

The one thing about being a waitress that Brinkley found strangely satisfying was the tips. She should have been outraged to have worked that hard, to have been put in a position of servitude for such measly remuneration. But it was the first time Brinkley had ever worked to earn anything, and though the tips were modest, she felt an unfamiliar sense of pride in the fact that they were hers. Well, Miranda's really. But sort of hers.

Otherwise, being Miranda sucked. And Brinkley wanted it to be over. She kept willing herself to wake up, but nothing happened. She wanted to be in her own body. She worried it might never happen. She wanted her life back.

She wanted her mom. She thought of how Miranda's mother had said "I love you" just before she—Miranda?—got out of the car. Brinkley desperately wanted to hear her own mother say those words to her today, to take her in her arms and make it all be over.

After she finished her shift, a busboy—whose name was Jerry, and who looked like more of a bus*man*, really—gave her a ride home. Brinkley had an idea. "Could you make another stop on the way?" She gave him the Harpers' address.

Jerry looked at her suspiciously. "What business do you have in richie town?"

"I just need to do something." Brinkley hoped her parents would be home by this time. Perhaps they were worried about her. It wasn't like her to stay out late without calling. Well, OK, it was . . . but maybe they were concerned this time. Maybe there was a parent-child bond that would lead them instinctively to know there was something wrong.

"I'm not robbing anybody," Jerry said. "My parole officer finds out you did anything and I was the one driving, I'm headed for the joint."

"You have a parole officer?"

I'm in the car with a criminal! Brinkley thought. *Beautiful. Fan-freaking-tastic.*

"Relax, man," he said. "I'm rehabilitated." She pointed out her house, and he pulled up to the Harpers' home. "You know these people?"

"Sort of," she said. "Listen, you can go now."

Jerry said, "I'll wait. I don't think this will take long."

Brinkley went to the door. She could see the light on in the den, and she could hear the hum of the television. She rang the bell. Cocoa started barking. She heard her mom call, "Someone's at the door! I'll get it!" Dr. Harper cracked the door open. Cocoa fought to wriggle past her, but she held him back with her foot.

Mr. Harper appeared behind his wife. "Something we can help you with?"

"Hi," Brinkley said. "How's it going?"

"Is there something you wanted?" Dr. Harper asked.

"Do you know where Brinkley is?" Brinkley said.

"What do you want with Brinkley?"

"Oh, nothing, really," Brinkley said. "I'm just . . . a friend of hers."

"Brinkley's not here," said Mr. Harper. "You must have our daughter mixed up with someone else."

"Yeah, there are, like, *tons* of Brinkleys in this town," Brinkley said.

"Don't get smart with me, young lady. You have no business here. If it's drug money you're after, you've come to the wrong place," Mr. Harper said.

"Walter —"

"I'll handle this, Charla. Look, get out of here now, or we'll call the police."

Just then, Cocoa broke free and attacked Brinkley with gleeful licking. "Cocoa, get back here now!" said Dr. Harper.

Mr. Harper jerked him back by his collar. "What's gotten into you?" he said. Then he turned his attention back to Brinkley. "Go on, now. And don't come back."

"But, Mom—" Brinkley said, just before her father slammed the door in her face.

Stunned, Brinkley stood motionless. She could hear her mom saying, "She thought I was her mother," and her dad replying, "Obviously a drug addict! All those piercings. . . . No one sober would look like that."

Jerry dropped Miranda at her house. But instead of going through the door, Brinkley sneaked behind the house to her bedroom window. One smooth shove and it opened without a sound. She climbed through.

Brinkley went to the shrine area and picked up a book of matches. As she lit the candles and watched them glow in the darkness, she thought she understood why Miranda had created the little sanctuary. Rejection was an unpleasant feeling. But perhaps it wasn't as new to Brinkley as she'd wanted to believe. Her parents hadn't seemed the least bit concerned about where she was so late on a school night. And they hadn't recognized their own daughter. Brinkley had thought they would at least sense that she was their own flesh and blood, even if she were inhabiting a different body. Or were they simply too preoccupied with their own lives to notice?

Brinkley kicked off her black tennis shoes and sat back on the bed. Her legs and back ached from her shift. The last thing she remembered was thinking that she'd rest her eyes for just a minute.

Brinkley woke up at home in her own bed. Her mother was turning on a lamp.

"Mom!" Brinkley said, jumping up and throwing her arms around her mother.

"Careful, you'll muss my hair," said Dr. Harper. "I've got a plane to catch and no time to fool around. Where's your beach tote? I need to borrow it."

"Oh, Mom, I'm so glad you're here. I had a terrible dream," Brinkley said.

Her mother didn't seem to hear her. "Oh, here it is. You don't mind, do you?"

"You're going somewhere?"

"Don't you remember? Your father and I are off to Bora-Bora for a couple of weeks."

"No, I don't remember!" Brinkley said. She sat back down on the bed, fighting a sudden urge to throw herself on the floor and kick like a toddler.

"Honey, I told you about it months ago. A pharmaceutical company is hosting a convention, and your dad and I decided to stay on longer for a vacation. Don't worry, we'll bring you back something fabulous!"

Cocoa bounded into the room and jumped into Brinkley's lap, licking her face.

"Cocoa! Get down!" Dr. Harper said. "Brinkley, don't let the dog lick your face. It's disgusting."

"It's OK," said Brinkley, nuzzling Cocoa. "Good dog, good dog," she whispered. "Mom, about last night...were you worried about me?"

"Of course not. Your father and I trust you. Oh, that counselor called—the one you have to see to keep from getting expelled. She wants you to come in first thing this morning. She said she's cleared it with the principal."

"An appointment during school? That's weird," Brinkley said.

"Whatever you have to do," Dr. Harper said. "An expulsion would keep you from getting into any kind of decent college. And that's just not an option."

"I know, I know." Brinkley followed her mother downstairs and said good-bye to both her parents. Her father rushed her mother out the door, reminding her of the time.

"Oh, and Brinkley," her father said just before they got in the car. "Make sure to set the alarm every night, and don't open the door to strangers. There was a suspicious character in the neighborhood last night."

The hair on Brinkley's arms stood on end. "Suspicious character?"

"Some drug-addled teenage girl," he said.

"Yes, do be careful," her mother added.

"Wait . . . what did she look li—"

"We'll have to talk later," her father said. "Just use your credit card if you need anything while we're gone."

As they drove away, Brinkley's dad honked the horn and waved. "I love you," Brinkley whispered, to no one in particular.

She sat at the breakfast table for some time, feeling strange, wondering about what her parents had said. Eventually, she decided she must have overheard their conversation with Miranda and incorporated it into her dream. She chose to ignore the fact that her room was located in an entirely different wing of the house, too far from the front door to have heard anything of the kind.

Brinkley reached the counselor's office at what would have been the beginning of first period. At least she was missing English. Given the twenty-minute drive from Irirangi's office to school, Brinkley reasoned that if she dragged this out enough, she might manage to miss all of her morning classes.

"What's the big emergency?" she asked the counselor. "Why'd you want to see me during school hours?"

"You missed our appointment yesterday."

"Yeah. So?"

"Let's talk," Irirangi said.

"About what?"

"I don't know. Is there anything you'd like to talk about?"

"Not particularly."

"Everything's going well for you?"

"Yeah."

"Nothing you want to discuss? Nothing at all?"

"I already told you, no."

"All right, then. At our last session, I showed you some photographs of different people and had you tell me what you thought of them. Today, I'd like us to look at you." She handed Brinkley a mirror. "Tell me what you see."

Brinkley gave a satisfied sigh. "Sheer perfection," she said, cocking her head and almost daring Irirangi to disagree.

"You are a very pretty girl," Irirangi said. "But is there anything else to Brinkley Harper besides being pretty?"

"Of course."

"Like what?"

"I'm also a fantastic dresser!"

"You know, Brinkley, beauty fades. You won't always be seventeen. One day in your thirties, you'll wake up and notice a wrinkle. You'll begin to see that your skin is less taut, that your eyes crinkle when you smile. Maybe you'll gradually put on a little weight here and there. You'll find a gray hair and pluck it out. Then you'll find several, and eventually, so many that you can't pluck them all out. What are you going to do then?"

"Botox, Pilates, and Redken," Brinkley replied.

Irirangi sighed. "My point, Brinkley, is that you can't rely on your looks to get you through life. At some point, you're going to have to think about the person underneath that exterior you're so enamored of."

"I'll worry about that when—and *if*—I get old and gross, like you said."

"That's a long time to wait to work on yourself, don't you think?" asked Irirangi. "I wonder what would happen if you didn't see such a pretty reflection in the mirror."

Brinkley said nothing.

"What? No witty retort?" Irirangi sat back and crossed her legs. "Could it be that you're actually taking this seriously?"

"Don't get your hopes up," Brinkley said. "It's just that . . . I have very vivid dreams sometimes. Last night, I dreamed I was someone else. It felt so real that I was actually kind of freaked out for a minute when I woke up."

Irirangi nodded. "Dreams can be a powerful force," she said. "You know, some cultures think of dreams as alternate realities. Some believe that when we dream, our spirits leave our bodies and mingle with other spirits."

The chimes near the window tinkled as a light breeze blew.

"Yeah, well . . . people believe all kinds of stupid stuff."

Irirangi smiled. "An open mind is a beautiful thing, Brinkley."

chapter eleven

*B*rinkley had given her the obligatory eye roll, but what Irirangi said about dreams had freaked her out.

A lot.

The dream about being Miranda had been *so real.*

When she got to school, everyone was in class and the halls were empty. She had the perfect opportunity to see just how real her dream had been.

She walked up to Miranda's locker, the one she'd opened in the dream.

Nothing was going to happen.

This probably wasn't even Miranda's locker. There were hundreds of lockers in the school, and she'd never noticed Miranda Morrison's.

But just to prove to herself that it had all been nonsense, she dialed the combination she so vividly remembered—4-22-32—and pulled the handle.

The door opened with a squeak of hinges. Brinkley gasped. Then she heard a voice on the other side of the metal door. "What do you think you're doing?"

Brinkley slammed the door quickly and saw Miranda staring at her. "Hey!" she said nervously. "What's up?"

"What's up?" Miranda scowled. "What's *up?*"

"Yeah, you know. . . . What's goin' on? What's shakin', bacon?" Did she really just say that?

"I'm morally opposed to bacon," said Miranda. "Therefore, please do not refer to me as the flesh of a slaughtered animal."

"Right. What I meant was, 'How are you, tofu?'" Brinkley laughed nervously. "Well, I'd better get to class."

Miranda grabbed her by the arm as she tried to walk away. Just above her knuckles, written in black marker, was the word REFUSE. Brinkley wondered if it was meant to be the verb, as in, maybe, *refuse to conform,* or the noun, as in Miranda had labeled herself as something that had been tossed aside. "You never answered my question, cheerleader," Miranda said.

"Your question? What question was that?" There was no taint of sarcasm in Brinkley's voice. Her heart was beating so fast that she felt sure Miranda could hear it.

"What. Are you doing. In my. Locker?"

"This is your locker?" Brinkley replied. "Well, that makes a lot more sense. See, I thought this was my friend's locker, and I was just, um, leaving her a note, and I guess I picked the wrong one."

"Then how'd you know the combination?"

"The combination. Yes. Good question. I don't know. I guess I just got lucky?"

The bell rang. Miranda said, "I don't know what you're up to, but if I were you, I'd see that my luck changed."

chapter twelve

$\mathcal{W}$hen Wednesday and Thursday passed without incident, Brinkley was able to convince herself that she had imagined the whole thing about becoming Miranda. It *had* to have been a dream. The fact that she'd known Miranda's combination was just some weird coincidence. She'd read about things like that on the Internet. They probably just happened sometimes.

Now that she had pushed aside the notion that something so awful could have actually occurred, Brinkley woke up on Friday morning feeling tough and defiant. She decided that the look for the day would be moxie-chic, à la Faye Dunaway in *Bonnie and Clyde*. She topped off her fitted, belted sweater and khakis with a black beret—an accessory none of the other girls would have dared—and ballet slippers. It worked. She looked in the mirror and pouted her lips. A little extra blush just under the cheekbones and her features were perfectly chiseled. She was every bit the cool, blonde goddess that was Dunaway.

But her pants felt tight. Strange.

"You need to watch your salt intake," was the first thing Bette said when Brinkley got to school that morning. "You're seriously bloated."

"I knew it!" Brinkley replied. "What is up with that?" Still, it was just a little bloating, nothing to be overly concerned about. She'd definitely watch the salt, though. "Must be PMS." Yeah, that had to be it. Because in addition to being bloated, Brinkley just didn't feel like herself.

And that was just scary.

Still, she was going with the it-was-all-a-dream plan. *Push it out of your head,* she told herself. *There's no way any of that could have really happened.*

For most of the day, Brinkley chewed gum—a nervous-energy activity and a way to keep from eating, because she was *so* not going to get any more bloated—but she knew better than to try to get away with it in Ms. Ouderkirk's class. Before the bell rang, Brinkley discreetly took out her gum and pushed it onto the underside of the lab table.

"Um, gross," Matt said. "Someday, somebody's going to have to clean that up."

"But not me," Brinkley said lightly.

"You're terrible, you know that?" Matt shook his head. "Did you read the chapter on sound waves? Wait—don't tell me. I'm going to go with either, 'No, are you kidding me,' or a three-syllable 'Please,' followed by an eye roll."

"Actually, I did."

Matt eyed her quizzically. "Have we met?" he said, extending his hand. "I'm Matt Baker. Welcome to Story High."

"Hey, I'm not illiterate!" Brinkley teased. "Just generally uninterested and uninspired."

"So what's different?"

"I was just thinking about how you said science can explain the unexplainable. So I gave it a shot and read it during English this morning. But I didn't really get it. Can you explain it to me?"

Matt grinned. "What am I, your slave? Why should I do all the work for you?"

"Because I'm the swellest lab partner ever!" Brinkley said, cocking her head to one side in the flirtatious way she'd learned long ago would get a guy to do anything she asked. "Besides, none of this stuff makes any sense without your help." She attempted to twist the ring on her finger, but found that it was a bit tighter than usual.

"Well, it is true you'd be lost in this class without me," Matt said. "OK, here's the gist of it: A wave is a disturbance. I hit my hand on the table, like so, and it creates a noise because I've disrupted the environment. Waves have to travel through a medium in order to transport the energy from one location to another—in this case, from the table to your ear. Now, a medium is the thing, in this case, interactive particles, through which the waves are moving, so —"

"Medium! Like Whoopi Goldberg in the movie *Ghost?*" Brinkley was suddenly intrigued.

"That's not exactly what I had in mind. . . ."

"But in the movie, Whoopi is somebody else, right? Patrick Swayze passes through her body like one of these waves you're talking about?"

"And this relates to physics how, exactly?"

"Well, your point is that waves of energy or whatever can pass through one medium to another. So does that happen in real life?"

"Of course it happens in real life. If it didn't, you wouldn't be able to hear anything. Sound waves pass through the medium of—"

"No, not that boring stuff. I mean, like, can a person become a wave of energy and interact with the atoms of another person?"

"Are you feeling all right, Brinkley?"

"Like, can you sort of . . . share atoms with someone else . . . for a little while?"

"I don't know, but that would make a great pick-up line at a nerd party." He leaned toward her and said in a low voice, "Hey, baby. Wanna combine our atoms?"

"Matt, I'm serious!" Brinkley said, though she couldn't help but laugh. "Can you, or not?"

"No—I mean, I don't think so."

"Are you sure?"

"If I understand what you're asking, it sounds like maybe you're getting at stuff like quantum entanglement. Purely sci-fi."

"But what if it's not purely sci-fi—what if whatever you just said is possible in the real world? Things—or people—getting tangled up?"

"Brinkley, do you realize that quantum physics is an extremely difficult area of science? Lots of people with PhDs don't even understand this field. I have only the most basic grasp of the very tip of the iceberg—and that's mostly from watching *Star Trek,* not from actually studying it. Are you really interested in this?"

"Extremely!" Brinkley replied.

"Well, OK . . . *theoretically,* there's such a thing as teleportation. Sci-fi writers have used it forever. It's when you scan an object to extract its information and then you send it somewhere else, kind of like a fax except it's the real thing instead of a copy. Like in *Star Trek* when they beam up."

"But instead of sending that information to a different place, can you send it into another person?"

"Come here," Matt said. He sat at one of the classroom computers and typed, "Einstein entanglement" into the search engine. He chose the first hit, a document titled "Einstein-Podolsky-Rosen Effect," and brought up a diagram with wiggly lines labeled A, B, and C. Two of the lines coiled together at the bottom like a rope and then veed out in separate directions. "This is really heavy stuff,"

Matt said. "I've heard about it a little bit, but I've never really studied it. My guess is that even Ms. Ouderkirk would be in over her head with this. It's unbelievably complex."

If there were a scientific explanation, however theoretical, for her Miranda experience, maybe it hadn't been a dream after all. "Do you think you could make any sense of it?" she asked.

"I don't know. Maybe. If I studied it enough, I might be able to get a basic idea."

"Hey—do you think we could study it together after school?"

Matt blushed. "You want to get together after school? With me?"

"Absolutely! Can you meet me in the library after my seventh-period cheerleading practice?"

"Can I meet you after your cheerleading practice?" Matt said the words slowly, as though this were his first and probably only opportunity ever to hear them. "Yes. Yes I can."

"Great!" Brinkley said, excited. "I can't wait!"

When Brinkley later told Bette and Tristan that she was meeting Matt Baker after practice instead of hanging out with them, they weren't so much affronted as perplexed. "Matt Baker? That dork guy?" Bette asked. "Why?"

"He's helping me with physics," Brinkley said. Then, seeing the look on their faces, she added, "I'm totally tanking, and my dad will kill me if I don't pull up my grade. He's even threatened to make me quit the squad!"

"Just make sure Science Boy keeps his distance," Tristan said. Then he laughed. "Like I have anything to worry about, right?"

chapter thirteen

While changing into her shorts and tank for cheerleading practice, Brinkley noticed something shocking: when she stood in front of the mirror with her feet together, her thighs touched. Normally, there was at least a half inch in between. Sure, some of the other girls had legs with more meat, but not Brinkley. This was not in keeping with her image as an Audrey Hepburn gamine. She thought of what Irirangi had said yesterday, about how looks gradually fade. Could it begin at seventeen?

No more Cokes, no more carbs, she told herself.

At practice, Brinkley found that she was unable to perform the moves with her usual ease. When she kicked her legs over her head to do a back handspring, it required a level of effort she was unaccustomed to. There seemed to be more hips and thighs to propel up and over.

"Um, Brinks," Bette said, "what is up with you today? You are seriously sucking." The other girls giggled. "I mean, are you feeling all right?" she added. "I'm just concerned about you, that's all. You OK?"

"I don't know," Brinkley replied without really thinking. She looked down at her hands and noticed that her fingers were puffy and plump, and there were little dimples at the joints. The ring she'd tried to twirl on her finger in physics class now looked ready to burst off her finger. She took it off quickly. *OK,* she thought, *Cokes and carbs aside, nobody puts on weight this fast.* She didn't like where this was going.

"You know what? I'm going to quit for the day," she said. "You guys go ahead and work on the pyramid and the dance routine. I'm going home. I'll feel better tomorrow."

"You sure?" Bette asked. "Then I'll take over!"

School was almost over so, without even bothering to change, Brinkley drove straight home. She was there in fifteen minutes. Tallulah had taken Cocoa to the groomer and the house was quiet. Brinkley dropped her keys on the counter and collapsed, exhausted, on the couch.

A series of banging noises woke her: At first a louder one, followed by two or three smaller ones. It sounded like . . . cans falling from a soda machine?

Then there were voices. Girls' voices.

She opened her eyes and saw a messy locker room. She was lying on a bench.

Brinkley tried to sit up, but found that her body felt . . . different.

A sinking feeling came over her. She raised her arms to look at them. Her skin felt smooth as usual, but there was much more of her. OK, there was water retention, but this was something else altogether. She grabbed a handful of flesh around her waist. This was not her body. This body was at least a size—what? Eighteen? Brinkley had no idea what sizes big girls wore. She got up and looked in the full-length mirror.

She recognized the face looking back at her: Carly Myers. The girl Tristan had mooed at in the hallway on Monday.

"Carly, I didn't realize you'd still be in here. Are you feeling any better?" It was Coach Freedman, the lady with the short hair who wore jogging suits to work every day and actually seemed to enjoy coaching the girls' basketball team. "Your headache go away?"

"It must have," Brinkley said.

"Well, I wanted to tell you that while I appreciate the effort you put forth in PE today, it's really not necessary. A girl your size has to work up to a physical fitness routine. You don't want to overdo it."

"I'll keep that in mind."

"Look," the coach said, turning the two of them so they faced the full-length mirror. "I've dedicated my life to physical conditioning; it's what I do. We all have different body types. Your body is never going to look like mine, and mine's never going to look like someone else's. We just have to work at our own levels."

Um, condescend much? Brinkley thought. Was this coach actually suggesting that it was Carly's dream to look like *her?* At least Carly knew how to dress fashionably. She was wearing jeans that were a surprisingly good fit—flared at the bottom to balance out the heaviness of the thighs—and an A-line top, with a slim belt just below the breast to detract from the stomach. Even the neckline had been well thought out, with a delicate necklace creating a *V* to draw the eye downward and elongate the silhouette. Carly may have been heavy, but she knew her fashion.

"You're right, Coach," Brinkley said. "I'll probably never be able to rock that nylon jogging suit or that mullet inspired by Jamie Lee Curtis in *Perfect,* but I'll try to move past my profound disappointment somehow."

The coach seemed at a loss. "Oh, OK then. Good. Guess we'd better get to class, then." She pretended to be interested in reviewing some information on her clipboard as she left the locker room.

Brinkley stayed at the mirror, continuing to examine Carly. There was so much of her—enormous stomach, thighs, arms. And the chest! She couldn't believe those large packets of flesh just sitting there. She must've been at least a double D. They felt like bags of flour hanging around her neck. How did people move with these things? And to think that Bette's parents had actually bought her a comparable pair last year for her birthday! Brinkley looked in the mirror and held them in her hands, studying them.

"Um, why are you feeling yourself up in our locker room?"

Brinkley turned and saw Bette standing there with the other cheerleaders, staring at her. She let go of the breasts and stood open mouthed, unsure of what to say. It was bad enough that Bette had accused her of feeling herself up, but Brinkley was disturbed to think that perhaps she actually *had* just felt up Carly Myers. No, no, no. That totally didn't count.

Did it?

"Hel-lo? What are you doing in our locker room?" Bette repeated.

"I was . . . um . . . looking for something," Brinkley said.

"There are no doughnuts in here," said Bette. "No Twinkies or funnel cakes or anything else that might interest you."

Well, that was just uncalled for, Brinkley thought.

"I didn't do anything to you," she said. "Why are you being this way?"

Bette laughed. "Get your fat ass out of here," she said as she began nonchalantly taking her things out of her gym bag.

Brinkley felt her face grow hot as the other cheerleaders laughed at her. How humiliating! And what had she done to deserve it? Nothing at all.

"Where's Brinkley?" one of the other girls asked.

"I don't know," Bette replied. "Maybe Fat Ass ate her."

As the girls howled and high-fived Bette, Brinkley ran out the door.

The effort it took surprised her. It felt as if she were running through water.

No one was usually in the library after school, so Brinkley sought refuge in the back corner, where the old card catalogue was kept. She found herself shaking with emotion, and after one long, deep breath, she began to cry freely. This was an entirely new experience. She'd never been mocked by other girls before.

"Hi, Carly." The voice startled Brinkley out of her train of thought. It was Matt.

"Matt! Hi, Matt!" She couldn't remember ever having been so glad to see someone. Kind, sweet Matt. She wanted to hug him.

"You all right?" Matt asked.

She wiped her eyes. "It's nothing. Just some cheerleader . . ."

Before she could finish, Matt said, "Rule one of high school: Never trust a cheerleader. I learned that the hard way."

Brinkley gasped. She was supposed to meet Matt here after practice!

"If it makes you feel any better about whatever they did or said to you," Matt said, "Brinkley Harper asked me to meet her here, then stood me up like the chump that I am."

"Oh, um . . . I forgot to tell you that Brinkley asked me to tell you that she was sorry she couldn't make it."

Matt looked skeptical. "Brinkley told you to tell me that?"

"Yeah. She wasn't feeling well."

"No offense, Carly, but since when are you and Brinkley so tight?"

A voice called, "Hey, you. Dork Boy!" It was Tristan, and Bette was with him.

"What did you say?" Matt said.

"You heard me. Where's my girlfriend?"

Brinkley saw Matt's jaw tighten. "How am I supposed to know? She's *your* girlfriend."

"Yeah, well, she isn't answering her phone, and she was going to meet you this afternoon. What'd you do? Go all serial killer on her?" Tristan found his little joke hilarious. Brinkley did not appreciate his amusement at the idea of her untimely death.

Matt scowled. "I haven't seen her. She didn't show up."

Bette squealed. "I knew it! She played the Science Boy! She stood him up! Oh, thank you, thank you! I knew Brinks hadn't gone native. She totally dissed him!"

"You know how she loves to play with losers," Tristan said. "That's so hot."

"No! That's not what's going on!" Brinkley insisted. "She wouldn't do that! Not to Matt, anyway."

"Tristan," Bette said, "did you just see that? Talking livestock!"

"I've never seen one dressed up like a human before, either!" Tristan replied.

"Hey!" Matt said.

"Hey what?" Tristan said.

"That's not necessary."

"You want to make something of it?" Tristan said.

Really original, Brinkley thought.

"Come on, Tristan," said Bette. "Let's take your car and go look for Brinks."

Tristan pulled back a punch and stopped just before Matt's face, watching him flinch. Then he laughed, and he and Bette left the library.

Matt just stood there, the same stoic look on his face. "You don't really believe them, do you?" Brinkley asked. "They're such idiots. Brinkley wouldn't do that. I'm sure something important . . . something unavoidable . . . must have come up. If she's not sick, then I'm sure there's some other good explanation."

"Yeah," Matt said. "Because girls like Brinkley make plans with guys like me all the time."

"Matt—"

"You heard what they said. People like that play games with people like us. It's just what they do. See you, Carly."

He tossed his backpack over one shoulder and left the library. Brinkley wanted to call his name and explain to him . . . what?

How could she explain to Matt what she couldn't explain period.

chapter fourteen

Carly's ride home from school was her brother, Josh, who had graduated the previous year. Josh was one of those guys Brinkley had never actually talked to but was nevertheless aware of. He'd cultivated a pronounced disdain for school spirit and popularity that had put him on the cheerleaders' radar as a bad boy. And though Josh wasn't exactly good looking, there was something about him. He was lanky and pale and had a big, crooked nose kind of like Owen Wilson's. Today, he was wearing a long-sleeved tee under a faded black vintage one that said, "Cheap Trick" about twenty times down the front in white letters.

"I'm in a hurry," he told her as she got in the car.

Josh's rush to get to wherever he was going reminded Brinkley that she was supposed to meet with Irirangi after school. Obviously, that would be impossible. How was she ever going to finish these stupid sessions if she kept person-jumping?

Josh continued. "The guys are waiting at the house. We're having an extra practice because we got a gig at some bonehead frat party this weekend. Pay's good, though."

"So you're practicing at your—our—house, then," she replied. Maybe she could look up Irirangi's number and call from Carly's home phone.

"Duh," Josh replied. "And before you ask, yes, Aidan will be there. He's kind of the drummer. But leave him alone, OK? I've told you: he's not interested."

Not interested? That was a new one for Brinkley. Whether she was in Carly's body or not, she chafed at the suggestion that a guy would be immune to her charms. Josh had thrown down the gauntlet. Brinkley adjusted Carly's bangs in the side mirror.

They pulled up to a house on a large lot. A small cement outbuilding sat next to the main house. Josh parked beside two other cars. "I'm just saying. It'd be better if you played it cool."

"I have to make a call," said Brinkley, "but after that, do you mind if I come and listen for a while?"

Josh sighed. "Suit yourself."

Brinkley looked up Irirangi's number and called to reschedule. When Irirangi asked why her voice sounded different, Brinkley told her she had a cold. Irirangi insisted that they meet the next day—a Saturday. *Great, another Saturday,* Brinkley thought. She hung up and looked for Carly's room so she could freshen her makeup and fluff her hair.

Carly's bedroom was easy to pick out: It was pink and black with girly accessories. Even her computer had a pink polka-dot frame around the screen. Brinkley couldn't resist. She sat down at Carly's computer and moved the mouse so that the screensaver— a series of positive quotations such as "'Perseverance is failing nineteen times and succeeding the twentieth,' actress Julie Andrews"— disappeared and the desktop became visible. She had a shortcut to a positive-quotation-of-the-day website, another to a diet-and-exercise-inspiration website, and one to a site with random cartoons. Above them was an icon that read "Diet Journal." Brinkley clicked on it.

It was a calendar with all of Carly's meals and snacks, plus her exercise regimen, detailed for weeks in advance. Even the portions were noted, the type and duration of each exercise spelled out. The meticulous attention to detail and the level of discipline required to accomplish something like this stunned Brinkley. She'd always assumed that girls like Carly ate nothing but pounds and pounds of junk and sat around on the sofa all day. She'd always thought they deserved to be fat. She remembered the day Tristan had mooed at Carly in the hallway, and she got a sick feeling in her stomach. Brinkley closed the document. She didn't want to think about it anymore. She went to Carly's vanity table and applied some blush, flipped her head over, and brushed her hair from underneath. A little lip gloss as the finishing touch, and she was ready.

Josh was plugging in amps while three guys were crowded together on a dingy old loveseat, staring at a television set and fever-ishly pressing buttons on game controllers. "I own you, bitch!" one yelled at another, slapping high fives with the third guy. "You suck!" the owned guy replied.

"All right," Josh yelled. "Let's light this candle."

"Hey, Aidan." Normally, Brinkley would never have broken the rule about not speaking first to a guy she was interested in. But in this case, she needed to know which one he was.

"Yeah, hey." Aidan was the owned guy. He barely looked at her and immediately addressed his bandmates. "What'd you jackasses do with my drumsticks?"

Did he just diss me? Brinkley thought.

One word came to her mind: *UNACCEPTABLE*. Who did this guy think he was? She'd seen him before, but it wasn't like he mat-tered. He was barely even cute, kind of short—and didn't he go to community college and work at Subway? Who did he think he was, Travis Barker? Well, he didn't know what kind of girl he was dealing with. If Carly liked this guy, and Brinkley was inhabiting Carly's space for a while, then Carly was going to get noticed.

She sat on the loveseat while the band began practicing. She perched her legs across the seat, making sure to have one leg bent, which was visually slimming for anyone and particularly necessary given the current circumstances. She put her arms over her head and feigned a languid, sensual stretch. This move usually drove guys insane and really was to be used only when a girl felt especially in the mood to torment, but with Carly's body, it was a different experience. In this position, those gigantic breasts of hers were practically under her chin, and she could feel her bra straining uncomfortably under her armpits. OK, she thought. Plan B.

Carly had great hair. *Long hair drives guys crazy,* Brinkley reasoned. She pretended to pop her neck as she seductively threw her blonde waves slightly over one eye. Then she playfully curled one lock around her finger as she looked at Aidan and smiled. He glanced at her and looked quickly away.

You've got to be kidding me, she thought. *Carly isn't so bad. She's kind of pretty. She's totally plus-size-model pretty!*

Though she'd never had to try so hard before, Brinkley pulled out all the stops: she giggled at all of Aidan's stupid jokes (though he made them to the band and not to her directly); she applauded after their set, specifically telling Aidan that his drum solo rocked; and she even—yes, a last-ditch effort—asked Aidan to teach her how to play the drums. Had Brinkley been in her own body, any guy would have welcomed this invitation to touch her hands and put his arms around her. But Aidan merely said, "I can't teach 'em. I just play 'em."

At a loss, she asked the band, "You guys want me to bring you some sodas?"

Josh jumped on the opportunity. "That'd be great!"

She went to the kitchen and grabbed some cans from the fridge. The door to the little outbuilding was slightly open when she returned, and though the guys inside couldn't see her, she could hear them clearly. They were laughing.

"Shut up, man! That's so not cool!" Josh was saying.

"I'm sorry, dude, but come on!" another guy said. "It's so obvious!"

"You shouldn't encourage her, Aidan! She's only human, and you're so sexy!" said the bass player.

"Bite me, OK?" Aidan replied. "No offense, Josh, but you're going to have to put your little sister on a leash. I'm not into fat groupies."

"Are you into me kicking your ass?" Josh said. "Because if you call my sister fat again, that's what's gonna happen!" The room became suddenly quiet.

She opened the door. "Here are your drinks." The guys avoided eye contact with her. "I've got a lot of homework to do," she said. "Good luck with your gig."

She went back to Carly's room, threw herself on the bed, and began to cry. It was all so humiliating.

She pulled the covers over her face. She was feeling that same exhaustion she'd felt at the end of her day as Miranda. Before she knew it, she had fallen asleep.

When she woke up, Brinkley was at home, in her own bed again. It was Saturday morning.

chapter fifteen

*B*rinkley had never before realized that she attached her allure to something beyond her long thin legs, tiny waist, and pretty face. She had believed that her outward appearance was somehow a manifestation of her natural superiority.

It was like she'd been fed a steady diet of lies since she was old enough to read princess stories: Girls who were beautiful deserved to be. Their goodness radiated outward and made them beautiful, even if they were forced to serve wicked stepsisters and wear rags. The evil witches who locked the princesses up in towers or kept them from going to the ball were ugly inside and out. Beauty was not an accident of birth, but a divine gift bestowed on a select and worthy few.

Or, maybe not.

To go in one instant from Brinkley Harper, dream girl, to someone undesirable and ignored was nothing short of terrifying.

It would have been one thing for a hot guy to have dismissed Carly. But Aidan? Brinkley had always taken it for granted that guys like Aidan were looking at her, wanting her. It had always been white noise—until it was gone.

Brinkley realized for the first time that the power afforded her by her beauty was unfair and unwarranted. And that made her want to cling to it all the more. So she got up and showered early, spending an inordinate amount of time on her hair, makeup, and outfit—a pink miniskirt, pink heels, and fitted pink top. She had some errands to run: another stupid counseling appointment at one o'clock, but before that, more important matters. She was going to get some answers, and, come hell or high water, she was going to Subway.

She was surprised when the doorbell rang. Who would be at her house at nine AM on a Saturday? She hoped it wasn't Tristan. But then she decided that was unlikely since a) he never got up on a Saturday before eleven, and b) he was probably sulking because she'd stood him up last night. How was she supposed to know she'd be Carly Myers on Friday night?

Brinkley went downstairs and looked through the peephole.

It was Matt Baker.

She opened the door. "Matt! What are you doing here?" It was all she could do not to hug him.

Matt looked shocked and seemed to have to work to keep his eyes off her legs. "I didn't realize this was your house," he said.

Brinkley didn't believe him. She took it for granted that everyone at school, especially guys, knew where she lived.

"It's so good to see you!" she said. "You brought doughnuts over?" It was a nice gesture, but he was holding five boxes. That seemed a bit excessive for two people.

"No," said Matt. "It's the Physics Club doughnut sale. Remember?"

"Oh!" Brinkley said. "Right! I totally forgot!"

"What a shock," Matt said.

"Oh, Matt! I am so sorry about missing you after school! I was . . . um . . . sort of sick." Bette and Tristan had seemed fine with the flimsy explanations, but Matt wouldn't be quite so easy to dupe.

"You seem to have recovered nicely from whatever it was."

"I feel a lot better now," Brinkley said. "Thanks."

"You must've been gravely ill. So ill you couldn't even text me to tell me that you couldn't make it."

Brinkley tried to change the subject. "You want to come in and have some breakfast?"

"No, thanks. I've got doughnuts to sell."

"Wait!" she said. She grabbed her purse off the kitchen table, then returned to the door with a twenty. "Here."

Matt took the money mechanically and handed her four boxes of doughnuts. "Thank you on behalf of the Physics Club." Before she could say anything else, he turned and walked back up the drive.

"Matt!" Brinkley called after him. "Come on, Matt! Don't be mad at me!"

But Matt wasn't listening.

Doughnuts disgusted Brinkley. Glazed grease. But today, she sat alone at the kitchen table and ate two of them, touching thighs be damned.

She took the boxes with her on her errands.

"I'm sorry, miss. We don't open until eleven," said the hostess at Ireland's Kitchen, the same hostess, in fact, who'd been there the night she worked Miranda's shift.

"I'm not here to eat. I'm looking for someone. Here, have some doughnuts," she said, shoving a box at the girl. The cook came out of the kitchen, looking intent on kicking her out. "Hey, Rodriguez!" Brinkley called, "What's goin' on?" Rodriguez and the hostess exchanged puzzled looks as Brinkley pushed past them to Miranda, who was busily marrying the sauces at one of her tables.

"I now pronounce you Heinz and ketchup," Brinkley said with a giggle.

Miranda was not amused. "What are you doing here?"

"I . . . um . . . I brought you a box of doughnuts!"

"What did you do to them?"

"Nothing! I just bought some this morning and thought I'd drop a few by your work. You know, see what you were up to."

"Cut the crap. What do you want?"

Brinkley sighed. This being-nice-to-people thing was overrated. "Look, did anything weird happen to you this past Tuesday?"

Miranda thought for a moment. "I was sick on Tuesday."

"But you don't remember anything unusual?" Brinkley said.

"I already told you: no. Nothing unusual happened to me on Tuesday."

"I don't believe you."

"I don't care what you believe!"

"Fine," Brinkley said, "be that way. I guess you'll just have to wonder why you saw me opening your locker. Forget I asked."

"Wait," Miranda said. "What were you doing, opening my locker? What are you up to?"

"I asked you a question first."

Miranda lowered her voice to a whisper. "I remember being in school and then not feeling well. It started as a really terrible headache. I went home, but I'm not exactly sure how I got there. I have no memory of it."

"Is your bedroom beige with a lot of candles?"

"Yes." Miranda looked at her suspiciously.

"And your dad . . . or is it your stepdad? He's . . ."

Whatever guard Miranda had temporarily let down sprang back up. "What are you getting at? How do you know anything about me? What did you come here for? How'd you even know I work here?"

"I just do," she said.

"So I guess you're going to tell your prep friends so you can all come to the restaurant and make fun of me?"

"Why would I do that?" asked Brinkley.

"Um, let me see . . . because you're you?" Miranda scowled. "Look, some of us have to work for a living. And if that means dressing up in stupid uniforms and waiting tables and humiliating ourselves by singing and dancing Irish jigs, then we have to suck it up. It's something you'll never have to experience."

Interesting choice of words. Why would she put it that way? Brinkley's mouth fell open. "Wait a minute! Now it all makes sense!" she said. "You're toying with me! I'm not crazy! It was *you!* You're a witch!"

"What?"

"That's what all this is! Your little candle area with the religious symbols . . . it's some sort of freaky spell-casting lair. What'd you do—throw together some eye of newt and tongue of bat? Or was it a voodoo doll? How'd you do it?"

"Have you completely lost your mind? Who told you about my candles?"

"Don't play dumb with me. I know you did something—some mind game or hallucination. Some sort of witchcraft!"

"Look, insane school-spirit robot," Miranda said. "I didn't do anything. Though, trust me, if I knew how to cast spells, you'd have been turned into some form of actual-as-opposed-to-metaphorical vermin a long time ago."

"Then you admit it!"

"Admit what? That I wish I could turn you into a vermin? Please— I'd have to get in line behind most of the school!"

"Then why did I know that your locker combination is four, twenty-two, thirty-two?"

"That's what I'd like to know! How did you?" Miranda asked.

"Because of your spell!"

"What? You think that proves voodoo magic is at play? Come on—you went to the office and got access to the locker info while the secretary was on break or something. It's not exactly *Mission: Impossible.* Why are you messing with me?"

"I'm not messing with you! Something weird is going on here. I know your locker combination, I know what your room looks like. . . . I know a lot of things about you I shouldn't know."

"You sneaked a peek at my locker combo—big deal. And the room thing is just a lucky guess. You don't know anything!"

"I know you have scars on your legs!" As soon as the words were out of her mouth, Brinkley could see by the look on Miranda's face that she'd crossed the line—big time. "I'm sorry," she said. "But it's true, isn't it?"

"Who told you? No one at school knows."

"I haven't been spying on you, and these aren't lucky guesses. I know a lot of things about you, OK? And I'm not sure how. But you swear you didn't do anything to me—no hocus-pocus of any kind?"

"Brinkley, I am not a witch. I didn't do anything to you. I don't even know what you're talking about."

"I believe you," she said. "I'm not sure why, but I do. Look, something weird has been happening to me. Don't you remember anything else about this past Tuesday?"

"Nothing," Miranda said. "I was sick at school, and I slept through work."

"But you didn't."

"How would you know?"

Rodriguez yelled, "Morrison! This isn't social hour! Get back to work!"

"Keep your shirt on," Miranda called back. "She's leaving right now."

"Check your attendance record in the school office," Brinkley said. "Check your time card here. You worked five hours on Tuesday."

"That's impossible."

"Is it?" Brinkley raised one eyebrow without even consciously trying to mimic Vivien Leigh.

"Yes. And I have silverware to roll in the back."

Just as Miranda turned to leave, Brinkley asked, "You hate the jig?"

"What?"

"The birthday jig, the one they do here. You hate it?"

"Yeah. It's the worst."

Brinkley let out a quick, breathy laugh.

Miranda said, "What are you laughing at?"

"You don't hate the jig."

"Of course I hate the jig!" said Miranda. "Everybody hates the jig!"

"But you're not everybody," Brinkley said. "Check your time card and get back to me."

chapter sixteen

onfiding in Miranda might have been a bad idea but for two reasons: One, Brinkley had to tell someone or go crazy—and she certainly wasn't going to tell Irirangi, who might use the information to have her committed—and two, Miranda was a good confidante because if she told anyone, Brinkley could deny the whole thing. She couldn't tell Carly because Carly might have some credibility, but who'd believe a Goth freak over Brinkley Harper?

For the time being, though, Brinkley had other things to think about. She had to get to Subway before the lunch crowd. And what about Matt? How was she going to get him to stop being mad at her?

And why did she even care?

It was only 10:45 when she got to Subway, so she was sure to have her victim all to herself before anyone came in demanding a meatball sub. She checked her hair and lipstick in the rearview mirror and pulled her skirt up just a little shorter before she went in.

Good. There were two of them working, both teenage boys, and no other customers. She could practically hear them gulp as she walked in. Maybe she'd hiked up the miniskirt a little more than necessary, but Aidan was going to suffer, and not just a little bit.

"Welcome to Subway," said the other guy.

Brinkley smiled. "This place is really kickin' today, huh?" Panic swept the boy's face. *Yes, I just started a conversation with you,* she thought. *It's your lucky day.* This was going to be too easy. "I guess the lunch rush hasn't really started yet."

"Yeah," the guy stammered. "We're usually real busy at . . . like . . . twelve, but now . . . not really." Ah, stating the obvious. The average male was such a quaint life-form.

"So, what's good? I'm positively starving!" She put her elbows on the counter and leaned in.

"Um, well . . . the Philly cheesesteak is good," the guy said.

"Sounds yummy," Brinkley said, "but I don't know. Do you think my legs are getting fat?" She backed away from the counter and ran her hands down her thighs. Aidan dropped the cup he was holding, and both of them stared at her the way an alcoholic in rehab might look at a dry martini.

"N-n-no," the guy said. "You look . . . perfect."

Brinkley leaned on the counter and touched his arm. "Aww! You are so *sweet!* *Maybe I should take it down a notch,* she thought. *The point is to torment Aidan, not this guy.* "Hey, didn't you guys used to go to Story High?"

"Yeah. We both graduated last year," the guy said.

"I thought you looked familiar," she said. "What's your name? Jason?"

"Jackson," he said, noticeably pleased that she'd been so close.

"Right! And I'm—"

"Oh, we know who you are," Jackson said. "You're Brinkley Harper. Everybody knows you."

The poor, sweet guy doesn't even know enough about girls to play it cool, Brinkley thought.

"I'm Aidan."

"Yeah, OK," Brinkley replied, somewhat coldly. She turned to

Jackson and smiled. "I guess I'll go for the cheesesteak, since you say so."

Brinkley's phone rang. It was Tallulah, probably wanting to know if she needed to pick up the dry cleaning. Brinkley let it go to voicemail, but she pretended to answer. "Hey, girl!" she said. "I'm at Subway, getting a cheesesteak sandwich from Jackson. Oh, you know, he graduated last year. Total sweetheart. Remember him? Tall? Brown hair? Yeah, that's the one. Hang on a sec." Brinkley decided that Jackson deserved a little ego boost. She covered the phone. "My friend says you're cute." Jackson smiled and blushed. Brinkley uncovered the receiver. "Well, you should come by and say hi to him sometime. No, I still don't know. Hey, let me ask Jackson and this other guy. I'll call you back, 'kay?" She pretended to hang up. "That was one of my friends from the squad."

"She knew who I was?" Jackson said.

"Well, yeah!" Brinkley smiled. "Why wouldn't she?" *A little confidence on a guy goes a long way,* Brinkley thought. "Anyway, she needs a band for this big party, and we just don't know anybody good who's not already booked. You know any good bands?"

"I'm in a band," Aidan said.

"Really? You?" She wrinkled her nose.

"Yeah," Aidan said. "Why are you looking at me like that?"

"I don't know, I mean . . . you just don't seem like the kind of guy who would be in a band."

"What do you mean?"

"I don't know. So, do you sing or what?"

"I'm the drummer."

"Really? I thought drummers got really muscular arms—is that, like, a myth or something?" Aidan glanced down at his puny biceps.

Having someone mock your body kind of sucks, huh, dude? Brinkley thought. "What's the name of your band?"

"Vera, Chuck, and Dave," Aidan said.

Brinkley didn't remember anyone in the band having any of those names, and there was no girl in the band at all, unless she'd missed practice. Go figure. "Oh, wait . . . isn't that Carly's brother's band?"

"You know Carly?" asked Aidan.

"Well, yeah! She's only cool as hell! Isn't she cool as hell?"

"I guess," Aidan said. "I never really thought about it much."

"I didn't know you were in her brother's band. I guess she never mentioned you. Hey, do you know who she's got a crush on?"

"Who?"

"I don't know—I'm asking you!" Brinkley said. "My boyfriend's friend has it so bad for her, but she won't give him the time of day. I think she likes some jerk."

"Your boyfriend's friend likes her?"

"Yeah, but you did not hear it from me." Brinkley's phone rang again. Bette. She pretended again to answer while the call went to voicemail. "Are you psychic or what? Would you believe I'm standing here talking to some guy from your brother's band? Yeah. The little short guy. . . ." Height was the ultimate blow to a guy's ego. They were so freaky about that—every guy Brinkley knew added at least an inch to his height on his driver's license. "Adam. OK, I'll call you back." Brinkley put her phone away. "Carly says hi to Adam."

"Aidan," he said.

Brinkley paid for the sandwich. "Great chatting with you guys. Bye!"

On her way out, she looked back over her shoulder, just to make sure they were still staring.

chapter seventeen

*H*ow's your cold?"

"My what? Oh, yeah. My cold. It's fine."

"You recovered quickly," said Irirangi. "Have you thought any more about our last session?"

"Actually," said Brinkley, "I have."

"Really?" Irirangi asked. "I have to say, I'm a little surprised."

"Well, you made some good points. I mean, I don't know. . . . I suppose it's possible that I might not always have my looks to fall back on. Like, what if I were in an accident or something? Or changed in . . . some other way?" Part of Brinkley wanted to tell Irirangi exactly what she'd experienced, but she was afraid of being diagnosed as a complete schizophrenic. They'd put her on medication and stick her in an institution, where she'd walk around all day in a fog, wearing a bathrobe and drooling. No way. She couldn't trust this woman.

"You're really thinking about this, aren't you?" Irirangi said.

"Yeah, I guess I am."

"That's good, Brinkley. I'm very glad to hear it."

"So, what are we doing today? You want me to look at more pictures? I'll do better with them. I was kind of giving you a hard time before."

"No kidding?" Irirangi grinned, and Brinkley returned it in spite of herself. "I do want you to keep thinking about those issues we discussed last week. But today, let's talk about communication."

"OK. What about it?"

"Well, the reason you came here—at least, part of the reason—is because your communication with other people needs some work. Of course, we want to continue working on what's going on inside, because that's the basis of how we interact with the world. But let's spend some time today working on how you communicate with others—what you say, what you don't say, and how you say it. Actions, too, are a form of communication. Maybe as a sort of homework, you could spend one day in silence. Just observing. Listening. Freeing yourself from the burden of language. You might be surprised how just listening helps us open up to others and be our true selves with them.

"Has there ever been any time in your life when you wanted to say something to someone, but were afraid or unsure of how to say what you felt?"

Brinkley didn't have to think about that one long.

"The look on your face tells me there has been," said Irirangi.

"I think maybe I'd like to tell my parents something."

"And what's that?"

"I don't know."

Irirangi paused before nudging her. "Try."

A long silence passed before Brinkley said, "You know how, when you're little, you're going down a slide or turning a cartwheel or whatever, and you bug your parents about it? Like, 'Look! See me!'"

"Of course. It's perfectly normal for children to covet their parents' attention."

"Sometimes, I still want to tell my parents, 'Look over here. See me.'"

chapter eighteen

Monday at school, Brinkley found Carly in the hall. "I told Aidan we were good friends," she said.

"What?" Carly asked. "Why? How do you know Aidan?"

"It's not important," Brinkley replied. "But if he mentions it, go with it." Carly looked confused. "Just trust me, OK? And by the way, Aidan's totally not worth it."

"What's going on, Brinkley?" said Carly. "Why are you telling me this? What did you do?"

"Think of it as a favor, for no reason other than girls should have each other's back once in a while."

"Um, OK. Thanks. Hey, by the way—great shoes. Are those Gallianos?"

"Yeah, they're new. Thanks. I've gotta run." Brinkley couldn't think about Carly anymore right now. She'd been looking for Matt all day and hadn't seen him once.

She got to physics early, but Matt was categorizing bottles in the lab supply room.

"Matt," she said, "whatcha doin'?"

"Organizing," he said. He never even turned to look. She waited in the doorway for him to finish, but he kept working until the bell rang and Ms. Ouderkirk began lecturing.

Brinkley had never paid so much attention to a physics lecture before. She wondered what had suddenly spurred her interest: Was it a way of distracting herself from Matt's coldness, or was she hoping Ms. Ouderkirk might touch on some of that quantum entanglement stuff that Matt had talked about? Brinkley took copious notes trying to make sense of the lecture—all the stuff about interacting particles. Maybe after class, Brinkley could try to get more information from Ms. Ouderkirk—information that might explain what had happened to her. She'd have to be cagey, ask questions from a purely theoretical standpoint. As Brinkley pondered this, she was writing so fast that she felt sure her pen would create a spark on the page.

Until she noticed that she couldn't read her own handwriting. And it wasn't because it was messy.

Her notes appeared to be written in a different language, one that didn't even use the English alphabet. What was it? Arabic? Chinese? Korean?

chapter nineteen

ear gripped Brinkley. She began to feel lightheaded and nauseated.

She stumbled to the front of the room. "I think I'm going to throw up," she murmured to the teacher. Mrs. Ouderkirk directed Jae, who was sitting at the front lab table closest to the door, to escort Brinkley to the nurse's office. As they walked together, Jae asked, "OK?"

"OK what?"

Jae smiled.

"Oh! You're asking if I'm OK," Brinkley said. "I don't know. I guess."

Jae stopped suddenly and winced.

"Are *you* OK?" Brinkley asked.

Jae, recovering, smiled. "Ow. Head."

"Headache?"

"Headache," Jae said. "Now fine."

Jae deposited her with the nurse and left.

"You're looking a little green around the gills, honey," said the nurse. She sat Brinkley on a cot and handed her a plastic bucket. Brinkley didn't need to ask what it was intended for. The nurse took her temperature. "No fever," she said. "Still, seems like there might be some kind of a weird bug going around. You can lie down and rest until you feel better. Can I get you anything? They have ginger ale in the teachers' lounge. You want some?"

"Yes, please," Brinkley said. Once again, she felt the irresistible urge to sleep. She lay down on the cot and closed her eyes while the nurse went to fetch her ginger ale.

It seemed that only a few minutes had passed when Brinkley opened her eyes. The principal and a couple of teachers were standing over her, and the nurse was holding her head and shoulders in her lap. They were on the floor of the hallway outside the main office.

"Can you hear me?" Mr. Russell asked. "Look—I think she's coming to!"

"She's breathing normally and her pulse is fine," the nurse asked. "Did you bump your head? Just lie here a minute until I can check you over."

Brinkley looked at her body, and this time, she wasn't exactly shocked to find that it wasn't hers.

The skin on her hands was tanner, and her nails were unpainted. She put her hand up to feel her hair: it was shorter, only just covering her neck, and much thicker.

"I'm OK," Brinkley tried to say . . . but she didn't understand the words that came out of her mouth.

She pushed herself up and rushed into the restroom across the hall. From the bank of mirrors, Jae Song stared back at her.

"쌍," she said to the reflection. 쌍? What had just come out of her mouth? She knew what it meant because she'd thought it in English. But how had she managed to curse in Korean? It must be Korean. Wasn't that what Jae was? Or was she Chinese? She'd have to ask

Matt. But how could she ask Matt, as Jae, what nationality she was? That might be awkward. And would it even come out in English, anyway?

As an experiment, Brinkley looked in the mirror and said, "Prada's new spring line is sure to be a hit." What came out of her mouth was, "프라다가 출하한 신춘상품이 틀림없이 히트칠거야."

Out in the hallway, the teachers and principal had left, but the nurse was still waiting for her. Brinkley gave her the thumbs up sign and walked on before the nurse could say anything else. Brinkley headed for the library. Once there, she went to a computer and typed in "Korean newspaper." There were results for South Korea and North Korea. Brinkley wondered if those were different languages. Just to be certain, she tried reading them both.

Both versions looked like hieroglyphic to her.

This was absurd. There was no way Brinkley could be speaking a language she'd never studied and couldn't read. But, on the other hand, perhaps the ability to speak Korean—but not read it— shouldn't have been any more surprising than taking over another person's body.

Brinkley had to try to get her head around this. *Think*, she told herself. But how could she possibly understand what was happening, why, or how to make it stop? *Focus on the basics,* she told herself. *Like, what am I supposed to do in the next few minutes?*

She thought about hiding in the library and hoping this would all go away, but she knew that, eventually, Mr. Russell or some teacher would come looking for Jae. Maybe she could find some answers while going about Jae's normal business. But first, she'd need a copy of Jae's schedule and student-information sheet from the front office.

In the hallway, Brinkley saw Tristan leaning up against some lockers, talking to Bette. Although Tristan had never before struck her as the knight-in-shining-armor type, Brinkley felt drawn to the familiar and approached him, hoping that somehow, he might be able to help. She reached out to touch his arm and pleaded, "사람살려!"

Tristan looked at her with disgust, jerking his arm away. "Excuse me?"

"사람살려!" Brinkley said again, this time loudly, as though greater volume would make him suddenly understand. "저좀 도와주시겠어요!" Expressing the same idea in slightly different terms didn't help, either. Besides, she wasn't sure exactly what she expected him to do.

"No, you may not do my dry cleaning!" he said. Tristan and Bette walked away, laughing.

"인종 차별하는 이 개새끼!" Brinkley shouted after him.

"You're going to be fine, you know," a woman's voice said behind her. A familiar voice. Brinkley turned to see Irirangi.

"What are you doing here?" Brinkley asked in Korean.

"I don't speak Korean," Irirangi said. She smiled and put her hand on Brinkley's shoulder, then walked away.

"Come back!" Brinkley called, but Irirangi kept walking.

Once in the main office, Brinkley spotted Miranda. Rushing to her, she began speaking rapidly: "Miranda! It's me! I've changed into Jae!" But, of course, everything came out in Korean, and Miranda didn't speak Korean any more than Tristan did.

"Hey, Jae. How's it going?" Miranda asked, as though she were placating a mental patient. Then she turned her attention back to the secretary. "There must be some mistake."

"Hang on just a second and let me see what this young lady needs," the secretary said.

Telling the secretary "I need my schedule and student information" in Korean did not help Brinkley's situation. After a couple of failed attempts at finding the right words, Brinkley pointed at the filing cabinet labeled "eleventh grade" and tried to make her lips form the question.

"I think she wants her file," said Miranda. "Is that it, Jae?"

Brinkley nodded excitedly. "File!" she repeated. "Song." The secretary pulled it and handed it to her. She didn't even notice when Brinkley made copies of the schedule and student-information sheet. She was too busy dealing with Miranda, who was insisting, "I was absent part of Tuesday."

"Not on our end. You were present in all your classes this past Tuesday."

"But I was home sick!"

"You were counted present in all classes that day, and I even remember seeing you myself."

"When?"

"When you came in here and asked for your locker information. Don't you remember?"

Miranda's face, already ghoulishly white, turned a sort of gray. "No, I don't remember."

Brinkley said, "That's what I was trying to tell you!" but of course, Miranda just smiled at her weakly and walked away. Language Barrier.

In fact, no one in the entire school spoke Korean, except Jae. There was no possible way of speaking to anyone.

Jae's schedule told her she had AP Calculus next. At least this class would be about numbers. A universal language! There were only five other students—only the best of the brainiacs in the whole school, including Matt Baker.

When Brinkley saw Matt, she suddenly felt the urge to cry. And she did.

Matt came over and asked gently, "Jae, are you OK?"

Matt's kindness only made Brinkley cry all the more. "You're so nice to everybody all the time," she told him in Korean. Matt didn't understand, but patted her shoulder and said, "There, there," over and over again.

When the bell rang, the teacher assigned a page in the textbook. Brinkley wiped her eyes and looked at the assignment.

What in the world was this stuff? So many symbols she'd never seen before. So much for math as a universal language.

As the other students worked, Brinkley listened to the sound of pencils scratching softly against paper.

After a while, she felt someone staring at her. She looked up and saw Matt, who furrowed his brow and whispered, "Are you sure you're OK?"

Brinkley smiled. Sweet Matt. She hated to worry him, so she nodded and pretended to work on the math.

She wondered why Irirangi had been at the school. Was she looking for her? And why would she look at Jae like that and tell her she was going to be fine?

When school was over for the day, Brinkley looked at Jae's schedule to see if she was supposed to take the bus or if she caught a ride home. Wherever that was. The CARPOOL box was checked. At least it should be fairly easy to pick out Jae's parents in the carpool line, since there weren't very many Asian kids at their school. The Lee twins drove a sweet convertible, so she knew their folks wouldn't be picking them up, and while she saw a few Asian kids getting on buses, she—Jae—was the only one waiting for a car ride.

But no one who looked remotely Korean drove up.

She remembered she'd also pulled Jae's student-information sheet.

It said Jae was an exchange student.

And her host parent was . . .

Oh, no.

Linda Adams.

The crazy woman who owned that taxidermy shop downtown.

A moment later, she heard the boisterous honking of a fifteen-year-old station wagon. Linda Adams, a fiftyish woman who looked as though she bought all her clothes at the Salvation Army, rolled down the window of the shabby brown geek bomb and merrily shouted, "Yoo-hoo! Jae!" Brinkley's stomach jerked into a knot.

She muttered, "쌍" for the second time that day.

chapter twenty

$\mathcal{J}$ ae's host mother talked incessantly, so Brinkley made use of the fact that Jae wasn't supposed to understand English, tuning her out after about two minutes in the car. Mrs. Adams flashed her painfully large smile every few seconds and overemphasized words such as "school" and "fun." Brinkley wasn't listening at all until she noticed Mrs. Adams's exaggerated miming of someone rolling a ball and her stretching out the word *bowling*: "booooow-l-ing."

When they got to the bowling alley and removed their coats, Brinkley saw that Mrs. Adams had "Linda" monogrammed onto the front of her shirt and Adams' Taxidermy as team sponsor on the back. Linda Adams handed her an identical shirt with the name Jae embroidered on the front. "A gift from your Aunt Linda!" she said, beaming. Brinkley managed to push out the words "thank you" in English, and she realized Matt Baker had been right—Jae's English was very good. Her pronunciation showed no trace of an accent. Brinkley wondered if it had anything to do with her and the fact that somehow the two of them were inexplicably crammed into one person. Or did Jae always speak so clearly? Brinkley had never bothered to listen to Jae before, so she couldn't say for sure.

Soon, Linda Adams was joined by several other aging adults in their Adams' Taxidermy bowling shirts. Linda greeted each of them warmly and displayed Jae as though she were a new doll. They each put their faces directly in front of hers and said, "Hello, Jae," their mouths forming crisp vowels.

Brinkley quickly realized that one thing Jae did not excel at was bowling. But then again, she wasn't much of a bowler herself, and the two of them together, with whatever Wonder Twins powers they might have, couldn't knock down a decent number of pins. The score seemed to concern Linda, but she tried to remain encouraging, clapping and shouting, "Good try, Jae!" after each pathetic attempt.

So this was what Jae did for fun. No parties with teenagers her own age, no dates, not even hanging out at a football or basketball game. No girlfriends to cruise around town with, looking for cute guys, or to stay up late with, dishing the dirt at sleepovers. Jae had come all the way to America to study and hang out with geriatric nerds.

When she couldn't stand the bowling any longer, Brinkley said to Linda, "Homework?" Linda seemed to light up at the suggestion—an excuse for Jae to stop blowing the score. "You want to take a break and do your schoolwork?" Linda asked. Then she turned to her friends. "She's such a smart girl!"

Brinkley went to a vacant contoured plastic seat away from the crowd and unzipped Jae's backpack. Inside, she found an opened envelope with funky-looking writing and airmail stamps. Brinkley couldn't read a word of it, but there were photos enclosed, and she assumed these were pictures of Jae's family back in Korea. In one of the photos, a man, a woman, and a little boy—all wearing what seemed to Brinkley traditional costumes—stood in front of a brick wall. In another, the same people were dressed in regular Old Navy–type stuff. Brinkley wondered what Jae must have felt when she first opened the envelope and saw these pictures.

It struck her that Jae's family was even farther away than Brinkley's parents were now. She gently touched the paper that had been touched by Jae's mother, an entire world away, and felt a twinge of sadness.

One of the bowlers brought Brinkley a large slice of pizza and a soda, which Brinkley assumed must count for her dinner. Brinkley blotted away the pool of grease that sat atop the cheese and pepperoni with her paper napkin. Remembering her experience as Carly, she was at first reluctant to eat anything so highly caloric. But then she decided that maybe Jae would get the calories instead of her, so she took a big bite. *Heaven,* she thought.

An hour or so later, she heard Linda Adams say to one of her friends, "I really should get Jae home. It's a school night, after all."

Given that she'd never needed an animal stuffed and mounted, Brinkley had never before been inside Adams' Taxidermy Shop, a.k.a. Linda Adams's house. There was no garage. Mrs. Adams parked on the street, and they entered through the front door, where they were greeted by a small bobcat bearing its fangs and holding up a front paw. Mrs. Adams hooked her key ring on the paw.

"Goodnight, Jae!" Mrs. Adams announced. Brinkley smiled and wondered which room was Jae's. There were five closed doors along the hallway opposite the business office. Brinkley opened the first one, and Mrs. Adams said, "Jae, do you need an extra blanket?" Linen closet. Brinkley shut the door and tried the next one. "Sleep tight!" called Mrs. Adams, so Brinkley assumed she must have chosen the right door.

She turned on the light and nearly screamed when she caught sight of a grizzly bear standing on its hind legs, its jaws in a perpetual snarl. *Nice,* thought Brinkley. *Who's your decorator, Bindi Irwin?*

Brinkley sat down on the bed and wondered what to do with herself. She felt tired. Maybe she should just go to bed and hope to wake up as herself again. Her typical pre-bed routine would be to wash her face, brush her teeth, and apply a variety of high-end products to keep her skin blemish free. But there was no way she was using Jae's—or anyone else's—toothbrush, because that was just gross, even given the rather unusual set of circumstances. She decided to rifle through the closet, just for something to do, but that was even more depressing because Jae had only a dozen or so outfits, mostly knit tops, cargo pants, and lousy shoes. There was a computer running on the desk—a dinosaur with one of those gigantic tube monitors—but it was password protected.

Brinkley was unbelievably bored.

She lay down on the bed and closed her eyes. It was 9:34 PM.

❋

She awoke to a ringing cell phone at 12:01 AM. She felt normal again. She reached for the lamp next to her bed, and it was there. The light illuminated Brinkley's own room. She rushed to the mirror and verified that her skin had returned to its original milky color and that her blonde hair fell loosely about her shoulders.

Her cell phone rang again. She looked to see who was calling. Tristan.

"Are your folks asleep?" he asked.

"I don't know," she said. No way was she going to tell Tristan that her parents were in Bora-Bora. He'd invite everyone over to her house for a party—or maybe he'd just invite himself over, which would be even worse.

"I'm outside, parked just down from your driveway. Come on."

"What for?" she asked.

"Just come on."

Too freaked out about her recent out-of-body experience to think about what she was doing, Brinkley slipped on her coat and shoes, disabled the alarm, and descended the stairs, leaving out the back door. Tristan's car motor and headlights were turned off.

"What is it?" Brinkley asked.

"Nothing," he said. "Just felt like sneaking out. Where should we go?"

"Tristan, I'm tired." Brinkley closed her eyes and laid her head back on the seat. That did not stop Tristan from starting the car and speeding down the road, singing along with his Maroon 5 CD in an off-key falsetto.

"Tristan, you can't sing," Brinkley said.

"Why not?"

"No, that's not what I meant . . . not that you're not allowed, but that you can't."

"Huh?"

"Forget it," she said. She thought about when she'd seen him in the hall that day. "Do you know Jae Song?"

"Who?"

"She's an exchange student."

"What about her?"

"I just wondered if you knew her."

"I don't think so. Oh . . . wait. Some Chinese girl came up to me in the hall today. Maybe that was her."

"Korean."

"What?"

"Korean girl. Not Chinese."

"What's the difference?"

"Korea and China are not the same place."

"So? Are you half Chinese or something?"

"Korean! And no, I'm not."

"Whatever! Who cares?"

"Maybe you would care if you were Korean. And why were you so mean to her in the hall today?"

"I wasn't mean."

"You made a very insensitive crack about Asian people doing dry cleaning."

"What, did she tell you that? And so what? It was funny. If you'd been there, you'd have laughed, too. What is the matter with you tonight, anyway?"

Brinkley sighed. "I don't know."

"Well, you look kinda hot," he said. "Kind of . . . I don't know . . ."

"Disheveled?"

"Sure, I guess. Kinda messed up. Kinda . . . naughty." He leaned toward her. "So, you feeling naughty, babe?"

"Nope. Not even a little bit."

Tristan's hand made its way to her left thigh.

"Remove it, or you will find yourself an amputee."

"Come on, Brinkley!" His voice was back in the falsetto range. "You're supposed to be my girlfriend, remember?"

Don't remind me, Brinkley thought.

"This ice-princess routine is getting really old," he continued. "Any other girl at school would kill to be with me! Didn't you hear what Valerie what's-her-name did with Bill at that party last week? He'd never even *talked* to her before—and he's only second string!

Imagine what she would have done for *me!* Hell, she would've thought Christmas had come early!"

"Then maybe you should date Valerie what's-her-name," Brinkley said, no touch of anger in her voice.

"Yeah, right! Like I'm going to date that slut!"

This was how it worked with guys like Tristan: His desire for her was directly proportional to her unattainability. Brinkley was no fool—she knew the minute Tristan got what he wanted that he'd see her as damaged goods. But the fact that she found him mildly revolting kept that from happening. She'd be able to string along the school's most eligible senior guy at least until he graduated.

"Look," Tristan said, "you want to go somewhere and park or what?"

"I'll take the 'or what' option, thanks," Brinkley said.

Through clenched teeth, Tristan replied, "Fine," and roared the engine as he took a U-turn too fast. As he pulled into Brinkley's driveway, he said, "You'd just better think about it, Ice Princess. Lots of other girls would love to trade places with you."

Trading places. She'd already had enough of that for a lifetime. When Brinkley got out of the car, Tristan peeled out with a grand screech of the tires. "You are *such* a man," she muttered as he drove away.

Brinkley was too annoyed to go back to sleep. She poured out a bowl of cereal and turned on the TV in the kitchen. Tallulah had been watching C-SPAN again. A diplomat from Korea was speaking. After every few phrases, the voice of an unseen interpreter translated his words into English. Brinkley listened intently. She couldn't exactly understand what the diplomat was saying, but every so often, she caught a word or two.

Creepy.

When Brinkley climbed into her bed around one AM, she was a little apprehensive. There was no telling where she might wake up—or in whose body.

chapter twenty-one

The next morning, Brinkley was, to her great relief, still Brinkley Harper. No bloating, no black streaks, no speaking Korean. Still, she was way past trying to dismiss this as a bad dream, so she decided to attack the problem as rationally as possible. She went to her desk and made a list.

Events:
- *Black streak*
- *Miranda*
- *Fall asleep at Miranda's, wake up at home as me*
- *Bloating*
- *Carly*
- *Fall asleep at Carly's, wake up at home as me*
- *Korean writing*
- *Jae*
- *Fall asleep at Jae's, wake up as me*

OK, so maybe she hadn't paid that much attention in science classes, but it wasn't hard to see a pattern here: each instance had begun with a slight change, followed by a full-blown identity shift, and ended with sleep.

Next, Brinkley decided she'd have to find a way to take some control over the weird whatever-it-was-thingy that kept happening to her. She really needed a better way to refer to it—how could she describe it? More than anything else, it was like jumping into someone else's body, a *jump*.

She made another list.

Concerns:
1. Do they know I'm them?

She thought about that one for a minute. Miranda and Carly seemed to have no idea that anything unusual had happened. Jae probably wouldn't have either—though it was unlikely she could tell Brinkley or anyone else if she had. Brinkley crossed out that question. It didn't seem to be an issue.

2. Are they me when I'm them?

Probably not. While she wasn't sure about Carly, Miranda would certainly have taken advantage of a situation like that. She'd have done something horrible to Brinkley. OK, so she didn't have to worry about that. She crossed that question off her list, too.

3. Where am I when I'm someone else?

This item, Brinkley circled. Here was a problem. During a jump, Brinkley couldn't be wherever she was supposed to be, whether in class, at cheerleading practice, or meeting friends. And there were only so many excuses she could come up with before things could get really uncomfortable, like they had with Matt. Did her own body completely disappear when she was somebody else, or was it just kind of camouflaged underneath theirs?

Now that she'd identified her major concern, she had to figure out some way to address it. Until she could figure out what was going on, why, and how to stop it, she'd better have some coping strategies in place.

She logged onto the school's website and typed in her ID number and password. Then she clicked on "attendance record" and checked the days and class periods she'd been Miranda, Carly, and Jae. For each of those times, Brinkley had been marked, "ABSENT—UNEXCUSED."

This was a problem. Pretty soon, the principal would start asking questions about her skipping class.

And he wasn't the only one.

"So where have you been skipping to the past few days?" Bette asked when Brinkley got to school. "And why was I not invited?"

"What?"

"Come on," Bette said. "Spill it. Or at least you'd better come up with a good story fast, because Russell's gunning for you. He was trying to shake the rest of us down for info yesterday. But we played dumb, which was easy, actually, since we don't know anything."

"I'll take care of Russell," said Brinkley, though she wasn't sure exactly how she would. She figured she'd think of something.

It was during first period when the secretary buzzed Mrs. Nelson's English class: "Brinkley Harper to Mr. Russell's office, please."

Brinkley collected her things and went to the principal's office.

"Would you like to explain these absences to me now, or shall I call your mother?" Mr. Russell asked.

"I'd like to explain, Mr. Russell, but you see . . . I can't. It's kind of confidential."

"Then it looks like I will be calling your mother."

"Go right ahead. You have her cell phone information in your files," Brinkley said, hoping the cell service would be nonexistent at the resort in Bora-Bora or that it would be three in the morning there.

It was a good bluff. Mr. Russell dialed the number on speaker-phone and got Dr. Harper's voicemail. He hung up without leaving a message. "I can keep calling until I get an answer," he said, "or you could make this easier on both of us and just tell me where you've been."

While Brinkley struggled to think of an excuse, Mr. Russell's secretary buzzed his office. "Mr. Russell, excuse me, but there is another student waiting to see you."

"Tell him to wait."

"It's a her. And she says she has something urgent to share with you about Brinkley Harper's absences."

Brinkley's mind raced. Who would have any information about her absences? No one. Unless someone was making up a lie to get her in more trouble, and who would dare?

"Send her in," Mr. Russell said.

Miranda Morrison came in.

This couldn't be good.

"You have some pressing information to share with me, young lady?"

"Yes," said Miranda. "I know why Brinkley Harper has been missing class."

Brinkley felt her face get hot. Miranda had probably cooked up a way to get back at her for snooping around her locker.

"I'm listening," Mr. Russell said.

"It's my fault," said Miranda. "She's been helping me."

Brinkley almost interrupted Russell with his own question. "With what?"

"I'm a self-injurer," Miranda said. "Sometimes, at school, I have a hard time controlling my urges, and Brinkley's been helping me."

"She has?"

"Yes. She couldn't tell anyone about it because she didn't want anyone to know my secret. She's been with me, trying to talk me through my tough times."

"And I'm supposed to believe this?"

"If you don't believe me, you can ask the school counselor. She knows about my cutting."

Mr. Russell pulled up Miranda's attendance record on his computer. "But you haven't been missing class at the same times Brinkley has. How do you explain that?"

Miranda hesitated.

"Research," Brinkley said, jumping in. "I was, uh . . . looking up information about self-injury. Other times, I was on the phone with a hotline, trying to find ways to help her."

"And why would you do that? You're not exactly known for your compassion," Russell said.

"You're right," Brinkley said. "That's what I've been working on in those counseling sessions I've been going to. Helping Miranda is part of my therapy."

"Really?" he said.

"Yes. It was all the therapist's idea."

"In that case, I'll just step out and give your therapist a call right now. I'm sure she'll confirm your story—if it's true—which, to be frank, I highly doubt. You ladies wait here, and feel free to squirm while I'm gone."

When he left, Miranda said, "You're in therapy?"

"Never mind that! What are you doing?"

"Saving your butt," Miranda said.

"Why?"

"I checked my time card at work. Apparently, I worked a five-hour shift, even though I have absolutely no memory of it. All my friends say they saw me at school that day. They even said they had lunch with me. And I wasn't counted absent in any of the classes I missed, either. I just helped you out. Now suppose you tell me what in the hell is going on."

Brinkley paused. Maybe now, in the principal's office, wasn't the time and place to suddenly embrace complete candor with Miranda in regards to her bizarre situation. Still, it would be a relief to finally tell someone—especially someone who might actually believe her. She took a deep breath. "Tuesday morning, I woke up in your body—I was still me inside, but outside, I was you. I went to your classes, had lunch with your friends, went home to your house. Then your mom drove me to Ireland's Kitchen, and I worked your shift." It was a relief to get it all out.

"You mean you just . . . snatched my body away from me?"

"I didn't snatch anything! I don't even know how it happened. Don't you remember anything from that day?"

"Just that I had a bad headache. And a lot of sleeping. I had some weird dreams, but I thought it was some sort of short-term virus."

"What dreams?"

"I can't remember them. Just that they were unsettling. I felt kind of weird when I woke up."

"And when I turned back into myself, I slept like a rock," Brinkley said. "Like I've never slept before."

"You said you'd been three people. Who else?"

"Remember when Jae Song came up to you in the office and was trying to tell you something in Korean?"

"That was you?"

"Yeah."

"So, you couldn't speak English? How does that work?"

"Like I know!" Brinkley said.

"Who else were you?"

"Carly Myers."

"Really? Wow. That must've been different."

"It was. It's all been . . . different," said Brinkley.

"And you don't have any idea how you're doing it?"

"That's just the thing. I don't think I *am* doing it. It's like it's being done *to* me." Brinkley detailed for Miranda how each change took place, all the way down to the part where she made the list. "Matt Baker was telling me something about atomic entanglement or something the other day. It's when your energy waves or whatever get jumbled up with somebody or something else's."

"I feel so . . . violated."

"Sorry. It wasn't exactly a dream come true for me, either."

"He's coming," Miranda said. "We'll talk about this later."

Mr. Russell came back in. "I've spoken to your therapist. She confirmed your story."

"She did?" Brinkley asked. "I mean, of course she did."

"But from now on, if there's an issue during school hours, please let me know so I can adjust your attendance record. And please be sure to make up any work you missed."

They left the office. Brinkley said, "I owe you one."

"You owe me a lot more than one," Miranda said. "But who's counting?"

The two of them barely made eye contact at rehearsal. Brinkley ran lines while Miranda painted scenery. After everyone else left, Brinkley approached Miranda.

"Still freaked out?"

"No, I'm fine. Please, feel free to take over my body anytime." She shook her head. "I'm a little calmer, actually. But somehow, I don't think this is what Whitman had in mind when he wrote, 'every atom belonging to me as good belongs to you.'"

"What?"

"'Song of Myself.' Don't you remember it from English?"

"Oh, the grass guy? He doesn't happen to mention quantum entanglement, does he? That stuff Matt Baker was telling me about?"

"Yeah, right. So what else did Matt say?"

"He said it's purely theoretical and sci-fi, but he was showing me something about it on the Internet. Some arrows and letters and stuff that made no sense."

"We have to get him to explain it to us," Miranda said.

"I would, except that he's not talking to me. I was supposed to meet him after school, but I turned into Carly, so I couldn't show up . . . not as myself, anyway. Now he thinks I was just blowing him off and trying to make him look stupid."

"I could see you doing something like that," Miranda said. Brinkley glared at her. "I'm just saying. It's not that unheard of."

"Well, anyway, I told Matt I had a good excuse for missing our appointment, but I couldn't tell him what it was, so he didn't believe me. I don't know what to do."

"I'll take care of it," Miranda said.

"How?"

"Look, you can't exactly tell him that you teleported into someone else. I'll tell him you were helping me out with something."

"Like what?"

"You've got a car, right? I don't. I'll tell him that you're my ride to work."

Brinkley looked surprised.

"Come on, I know it's creepy for both of us that someone might think we're friends," said Miranda. "But you need an excuse, and that's sort of plausible. I mean, I don't have a car, and you do. No one else would believe it, but Matt would."

"Why would Matt believe it?"

"Because Matt thinks you're not really so bad . . . that you're just misunderstood."

"How do you know what Matt thinks?"

"He's nice to you, isn't he? I mean, except for now? He obviously prefers to live under certain delusions about your character. I'll tell him you were embarrassed to tell him. He'll believe it because he wants to. No guy wants to think a girl ignored him on purpose. The male ego prohibits them from thinking the worst in a situation like this."

"You're right, it is a good cover," said Brinkley. "But in case he checks up on it, there's only one thing to do."

"What?"

"Make it true. From now on, I'm your ride to work."

"Seriously? You're going to drive me to work?"

"And pick you up, too. I can't trust my only ally in all this to that criminal."

"What criminal?"

"You know, the guy who gave me . . . us . . . a ride home Tuesday. The busboy."

"What bus . . . wait a minute! Don't tell me you got in the car with Crazy Jerry! What are you trying to do, get me killed? Number one rule of Ireland's Kitchen is you never, ever get into a car with Crazy Jerry!"

"I'll keep that in mind next time I find myself in your skin," said Brinkley.

"Very funny," said Miranda. "Don't worry about Matt. I'll square things with him. I guess we might as well work together since you seem to know everything about me."

Brinkley looked at her. "Why do you do it, anyway?"

"What? Help you?"

"No, that cutting stuff. How come?"

"I don't know, exactly." Miranda looked away. "I read about it somewhere once, and I thought it sounded nuts. Then one day, when I was really upset and stressed out about stuff at school and things at home, I got a kitchen knife and tried it."

"Didn't it hurt?"

"It's weird. I guess I was more focused on watching myself bleed than on the pain. After I was done, I kind of felt more in control of my life. And so I kept doing it. "

"That's cuckoo."

"So are a lot of things. I'm working on it."

"I'm going to need a copy of your work schedule. Are you working tonight?"

"Nope. Free as a bird."

Tentatively, Brinkley said, "Well, I'm kind of freaked out, and I don't want to be alone. You want to come over?"

"To your house?"

"No, to the Yucatán Peninsula. Of course to my house."

"What for?"

"I dunno. My parents are out of town. You're the only one I can talk to about this. It's kind of scary. We could study. Or just hang."

Miranda thought a moment. "I guess it beats going home. Copacetic, then."

For a second, Brinkley thought, *What if Tristan or Bette or some of my friends see me with Miranda Morrison?*

Her next thought was, *Bite me.*

chapter twenty-two

 When Brinkley and Miranda drove out of the school lot, they didn't see Bette or Tristan or anyone else from Brinkley's usual crew, but they did pass Matt Baker. He looked puzzled as he returned their wave.

"That ought to help with the alibi for the other day," Miranda said. She picked up Brinkley's iPod from the console and scrolled through her selections. "I can't believe you actually paid for these crappy songs," she said. "It's not like they don't already play them incessantly on the radio."

"Oh, and I suppose your music is so much better?" Brinkley replied. "You could get that for free, too. Here . . . " Brinkley made a maniacal face and began screaming like a demon.

Miranda burst out laughing, which got Brinkley started, too.

"You've *got* to do that again and let me post it on YouTube!" Miranda said.

"Not likely!" Brinkley turned on the radio and hit the scan button. "There's got to be something on here we can agree on."

A few stations passed before Miranda stopped on the Smashing Pumpkins' "1979."

"Ooh! This one—it's a classic," Miranda said.

"Yeah, I like it, too." Brinkley smirked slightly when it got to the line, "hung down with the freaks and ghouls," but Miranda didn't seem to notice.

Cocoa began barking when he heard Brinkley's car pull up. "I have to warn you," Brinkley said, "Cocoa has to get used to strangers. But he doesn't bite."

When they walked inside, Cocoa leapt into Brinkley's arms and licked her face, shaking all over with excitement.

"Pooky wooky!" Brinkley said. Cocoa looked at Miranda and barked. Then he began sniffing with wild abandon. Next, he was in Miranda's arms, licking her face.

Brinkley said, "This is so weird!"

"What can I tell you? Dogs tend to respond to me better than humans do."

"But he's never like this with strangers! He still growls at Bette, and she's been over here a zillion times!"

"Animals can sense evil, you know."

"Oh, stop!" Brinkley laughed. "It's probably because he recognized you from that night I came by the house when I was you." She paused. "OK . . . weirdest, sentence, ever." She put down her keys and called Tallulah into the kitchen. "Tallulah, this is Miranda," Brinkley said. Tallulah stared. "Say hello, Tallulah!"

"Nice to meet you," Tallulah said to Miranda. "Miss Brinkley, will your friend be staying for dinner?"

Brinkley looked at Miranda. "Tallulah's a good cook."

Miranda shrugged. "OK, sure, I guess. Thanks." As the two of them walked upstairs to Brinkley's room, Miranda whispered, "Don't pretend you didn't just enjoy shocking your housekeeper."

"Yeah, well, don't flatter yourself. You're not *that* scary. You want to see Tallulah shocked, you should've seen her the morning after my spring break party last year. She found the band's bass player passed out in one of the showers upstairs. Now *that* was shocked."

Miranda looked around Brinkley's room. "Nice digs. Your folks must be pretty loaded, huh?"

"My mom's a doctor and my dad's a lawyer."

"What kind of doctor is she? A plastic surgeon?"

"How'd you know?"

"Lucky guess. What kind of law does your dad practice?"

"Divorce and family. He's tops. A lot of the richest people in town use him to draw up their wills or do some sort of paperwork for them, just so he'll have a conflict of interest representing their spouses if they ever get divorced. He's a real shark."

"So they don't spend a lot of time with you, huh?"

"My parents adore me." Brinkley grabbed a notebook off her desk and plopped down on the floor.

"You don't have to get all defensive. . . . I just meant that it explains a lot about you. Like maybe why you're so into material things. You know, the poor-little-rich-girl story."

Brinkley looked Miranda directly in the eye. "Are you sure you want talk about how parents screw us up? Because we could probably spend a good bit of time on your stepdad."

"I guess I deserved that."

"Sorry. I didn't mean to—"

"It's all right," said Miranda. "My stepdad . . . well . . . he drinks. A lot. And when he's drunk, he . . ."

"You don't have to say any more," Brinkley said. There was a silence between them for a few seconds before Brinkley said, "Let's get down to business, shall we?"

Miranda seemed relieved. "Right. Business. And what, exactly, is our business?"

"Weird person-jumping phenomenon?" Brinkley said. "And what we're going to do about it?"

"How did this become a 'we' problem, exactly?"

"Do you want me jumping into your skin again and taking over your body?"

"I can't even think about it. Way beyond the heebs." Miranda shivered. "Let's go over what we know."

Brinkley pulled a piece of paper out of the notebook and handed it to Miranda, along with a pen and a textbook to put under it. Then she reached into her desk drawer and pulled out the list she'd created. She set the paper between them, and Miranda studied it.

"OK, so the day you were me, I don't remember any of it. All I remember is getting a headache and then sleeping deeply for a long time."

"And you fell asleep in class and woke up in your own bed, but you don't remember how you got there?" asked Brinkley.

"Yes."

Brinkley made a note of it. Then Miranda asked, "So, if there are two people in one body, where's the extra body?"

"What do you mean?" asked Brinkley.

"I mean, where does your body go when you're them—us? It's not like you run into yourself in the hall. So where's your body?"

"I don't know," Brinkley replied. "I think it's still there. Just underneath the other person's. I mean, it's my brain—it's me, but it's like I'm in disguise. Does that make any sense?"

"No, but nothing about this does. Hand me your laptop." Brinkley obeyed. "Sweet mother, does everything have to be pink?"

"What's wrong with pink?"

"Nothing . . . except it's so . . . pink." Miranda typed *punnet square* in Wikipedia. "Don't you remember this stuff from ninth-grade biology?"

"Oh, yeah. I kind of liked drawing those."

Miranda read: "The way in which the B and b alleles interact with each other to affect the appearance of the offspring depends on how the gene products interact . . . blah blah blah . . . the dominant allele will mask the recessive one."

"They're talking about the color of a rat's fur," said Brinkley. "What are you getting at?"

"Maybe nothing. But I'm thinking that maybe, in this case, you've got two sets of DNA, simultaneously existing in one body, right? And maybe the other person's DNA dominates yours—at least in terms of physical appearance—like big B trumps little b, brown eyes mask blue. And that's why nothing about you is visible. Does this have anything to do with the science stuff Matt was talking about?"

Brinkley said, "I don't think so. But we need something to work with—some sort of parameters or some way to think about it." She rolled her eyes and scoffed. "Matt Baker is so wrong."

"About what?"

"He always says that science can explain everything in the universe. He should try this one!"

"Don't give up yet," said Miranda. "Look, there are certain rules that govern the universe, but that doesn't mean that we can understand all of them."

"Sounds like what Matt says—except Matt says you can understand them if you try hard enough."

"You pay an awful lot of attention to what Matt says, don't you?"

"Under these circumstances, you would too." Brinkley leaned back against her desk. "Miranda, I'm scared. What if this happens again? What if it happens in front of people? Or what if I don't turn back into me?"

"If it happens again, you can call me . . . or tell me, if we're at school. I don't suppose I can do anything about it, but I'll help you any way I can. It might be less scary if you can share it with someone else. Even if she is a Goth freak."

"You're not really such a freak," Brinkley said. "You just look like one."

Miranda laughed. "Thanks! That's really sweet of you!" She grabbed a stuffed dog from Brinkley's bed and threw it at her. Brinkley threw it back.

They were laughing when the door opened.

"What. In the hell. Is going on?"

chapter twenty-three

*B*rinkley looked up. "Bette! What are you doing here?"

"I was looking for my best friend, who hasn't been returning my voice mails and who I've barely seen lately. What are *you* doing?"

"Oh, um . . . you know Miranda?"

"Yeah," Bette said. "I know she's a freakbag who's seriously not in your league, so what's she doing here?"

"Bette—" Brinkley began.

"Save it, Brinkley," said Miranda. "Muffy Prepskie has a point. I'm outta here." Miranda grabbed her backpack and pushed past Bette.

"Miranda! " Brinkley called. "You don't even have a ride!"

"I'll walk!" The door slammed below.

"What is the matter with you?" Bette demanded. "You can't hang out with Goths!"

Brinkley rolled her eyes and sighed. "Why not?"

"Because it just isn't done!"

"Bette, I *so* don't care at this point what 'isn't done.' I've got bigger issues to deal with."

"Like what? What's going on with you?"

"It's complicated," Brinkley said.

"Does it have something to do with that Goth girl? What reason could you possibly have for dodging me and hanging out with her? Is she blackmailing you or something?"

"Of course she's not blackmailing me." Brinkley realized that the notes she and Miranda had taken were still lying on the floor. She began scooping them up, trying to act nonchalant. "You want to know the truth?" she asked.

"Yes!"

"Miranda is helping me with a project for English."

"Brinks, I'm in your English class. There's no project."

Good point, Brinkley thought. "Maybe not for you, since you're not failing."

"You're failing English *and* physics?"

"Please don't tell anyone. I asked Mrs. Nelson if I could do something for extra credit. Miranda and I are writing a short story together."

"Why her? She doesn't need extra credit. I thought she was kind of a brain in English. She's always answering questions in class. I never even know what she's talking about."

Another good point. "Yeah, well . . . she gets some community-service hours for helping me."

"Like you get for stocking that food pantry?"

I'm going to have to make a list to keep up with all these lies, Brinkley thought. "Yes. Like that."

Bette squealed. "She's a juvie?" She laughed wickedly. "You've *got* to tell me! What did she do?"

"I don't know all the deets," Brinkley said. She needed something to keep Bette away from Miranda. "But I'm pretty sure she stabbed a cheerleader."

Bette gasped. "Wouldn't we have heard about that? Wouldn't it have been on the news? Wouldn't she be in jail?"

Why was Bette so on top of it all of a sudden? "From what I heard, it happened out of town last summer—a girl we wouldn't know. And since she didn't die or anything, and since Miranda's under eighteen, she got probation and community service. And you wouldn't have read her name in the paper because they don't publish the names of juvenile offenders." She must've heard that from her dad or something.

"That makes sense," Bette said.

Thank goodness.

"But aren't you scared of her? What if she stabs you?"

"I can handle myself," Brinkley said, trying to sound tough. "But seriously, Bette, I'd lay off the insults if I were you. You never know when she might blow."

"Totally! Thanks for telling me, Brinks."

"Well, now you see that I was only trying to protect you."

"You are the *best,*" Bette said, hugging Brinkley. "Always thinking of others!"

"Always thinking of others," Brinkley replied. "That's me."

chapter twenty-four

*B*rinkley met Irirangi bright and early at her office the next morning.

"You lied to my principal for me," Brinkley said. "Why?"

"I didn't lie. He asked if your helping Miranda was a part of your therapy. I said yes. Anything that requires you to exhibit kindness to others sounds like an excellent step toward progress. And I have to say, I was very pleased to hear of your interest in this other student—a self-injurer, Mr. Russell said. Miranda, wasn't it? How did your interest in her develop?"

"Oh, well . . . I was . . . thinking about all that stuff you've been working with me on, about being nice . . . so I figured, who needs someone to be nice to her more than a freak, right?"

"Freak," Irirangi repeated. "One step forward, two steps back, as they say. In any case, good for you for helping someone."

"I saw you at school," Brinkley said.

"Did you? Why didn't you say hello?"

"What were you doing there? Were you checking up on me?"

"If I had been checking up on you, how would that make you feel?"

Brinkley sighed. "Do you always have to answer every question with a question?"

"All right, then. Let's say I was there checking up on you, just for argument's sake."

"OK. Why?"

"Because you're important to me."

Brinkley eyed Irirangi warily. "How come?"

"Why shouldn't you be important to me?"

"There you go again!" Brinkley said, but she followed it with a smile and a shake of her head. "So now I'm supposed to believe you're like my guardian angel or something?"

"Brinkley, is there something you want to share with me? Something about Miranda or the day you saw me at your school?"

Brinkley couldn't risk it. "No, I was just curious."

"To the matter at hand, then. We talked last time about communication, and I suggested some homework for you. Did you give it a try?"

"You mean where I was supposed to not talk to anyone for a day and see what that was like? Yeah. You could say I gave that a try."

"Really? Tell me about it."

Brinkley shifted in her chair. "Not much to tell. I just didn't talk to anyone much."

"Did you learn anything from the experience?"

Brinkley thought about Tristan's mean comments to Jae, and how Jae had no one at school to talk to, no one to understand her. "I guess it made me feel isolated." Brinkley wanted to ask Irirangi what was happening to her, whether she was going crazy, but she didn't dare. *Keep it together, Brinks,* she told herself. *Whatever this is, it will pass. You can't risk telling this woman. She could have you locked up.*

"Those are marvelous pants you're wearing," Irirangi said.

"Um . . . OK," Brinkley said. "Thanks."

"What did they cost?"

"Excuse me?"

"If I wanted to buy a pair of pants like that, what would they cost?"

Brinkley was taken aback by the rudeness of the question. "With sales tax and everything, probably about two-hundred dollars."

"Wow!" Irirangi said. "That's kind of pricey, isn't it?"

"They're Marc."

Irirangi stared at her.

"Marc by Marc Jacobs," Brinkley clarified. *And they're kind of not your style,* Brinkley thought.

"Oh, I see." Irirangi paused before continuing. "I'm just curious—did you buy those pants?"

"Yeah."

"And where does a seventeen-year-old girl get that kind of money?"

"My parents."

"So you earned the money from your parents?"

"I didn't come here to talk about my pants. And in case you don't know, it's pretty rude to ask people how much they paid for something."

"You seem upset."

"I'm not upset!" Brinkley said. "It's just that, I'm missing school for this session, and all you want to talk about is a pair of pants!"

"Missing school bothers you?"

"Yes. Yes, it does."

"You know what, Brinkley?" said Irirangi. "You're absolutely right."

"I am?"

"Yes. You should be getting back to school. And I'm sorry I asked such a rude question. It's just that . . . well, I really, really like those pants."

Brinkley didn't know what to think. This woman was way crazier than Brinkley ever would be, jumps or no jumps.

Irirangi signed a form for Brinkley to take to the school office and said, "You head on back to school. I promise that at our next session, I'll be more focused. And again, I do apologize."

"Don't sweat it."

Unfortunately, a pep rally had taken up most of the morning and pushed the entire schedule back for the day, so Brinkley hadn't missed her morning classes after all. Miranda confronted Brinkley at her locker. "You told Bette Caravallo that I was on probation for stabbing a cheerleader?"

Brinkley winced. "Sort of . . ."

"I can't believe you did that!" Miranda yelled. She put her hands up in the air and gazed at the ceiling, looking for the right words. "That is so, utterly . . . *awesome!*" She looked back down at Brinkley and held up her hand up for a high five.

Tentatively, Brinkley slapped Miranda's palm. "You mean you're not mad?"

"Mad? Are you kidding? This is my best day *ever* at this hellhole of a school! It's like parting the Red Sea when I walk down the hall, only with brainless preps instead of water. I actually slammed one of them into the wall and yelled, 'Move it, debutante!' Just like that. And nobody challenged me. They were *terrified*! It rocked!"

"Glad that's working for you, I guess."

"And it's not just your kind, either," said Miranda. "I have mad street cred now with the emos. One of them asked me if the rumor I'd stabbed a cheerleader was true, and you know what I did?"

"What?"

"I got all Michael Corleone on her! I said, just like this: 'Don't ever ask me about my business!'" Miranda laughed. "*The Godfather*. Ever seen it?"

"Does Luca Brasi sleep with the fishes?" Brinkley noticed a freshman JV cheerleader—Sara? Tara? —staring at her incredulously.

"Nice one, Barbie! I didn't know you had it in you." Miranda smiled. "You have no idea how much I love *The Godfather* trilogy."

"It's very Shakespearean, I think," Brinkley said.

"Wow . . . did you just say 'Shakespearean'?"

"We should have a *Godfather* marathon some night."

Sara/Tara was staring so hard she seemed to be trying to send a telepathic transmission into Brinkley's forehead.

"All right. So we can analyze Coppola's masterpiece after we figure out the solution to your problem," Miranda said. "If you jump again, alert me to the situation. See ya."

When Miranda was less than a foot away, Sara/Tara scurried over to Brinkley. "Didn't you hear about that girl? They say she stabbed a cheerleader!"

Brinkley felt amused at how quickly her story had spread. "Yeah, I heard."

"Well? Aren't you scared? You seemed pretty friendly with her." Sara/Tara stopped. "Oh! I get it! You're being nice to her so she won't stab you! Good idea! I'll bet if she kills the other cheerleaders, she'll probably let you live."

"Yeah. That's what I was going for."

Before Sara/Tara could say anything else, Bette appeared. "We're going to be late to first period," she told Brinkley, whisking her away. As they walked to class, Bette said, "Sorry again for yesterday. I've put all the cheerleaders on warning to stay away from Freakazoid."

"So I've heard," Brinkley said. "You know, Bette, it wouldn't kill you to be a little nicer to Miranda . . . and other people . . . even if you weren't afraid they were going to stab you."

"What are you talking about?"

"Just that, well, you're not very nice to people sometimes."

Bette looked at Brinkley in confusion. "Why would I need to be nice to a bunch of nobodies?"

"It's not a matter of need. . . . It's just common decency, that's all."

Bette pondered Brinkley for a moment, then burst into laughter. "Good one, Brinks!" she said. "You had me going for a minute!"

When they got to English, Bette took the long way around to her seat in order to avoid getting anywhere near Miranda, who didn't even notice because she was absorbed in a book.

"What're you reading?" Brinkley asked.

"Brinks!" Bette scolded, giving her a stern look.

"Would you just *chill* already?" Brinkley said, rolling her eyes. But before Miranda could reply, Mrs. Nelson started class. It was a lecture on modernist literature. Brinkley was about to doze off when the bell rang for second period. Miranda glanced furtively at Brinkley while zipping up her backpack. Brinkley gave a brief nod to indicate that everything was OK so far.

"I need to talk to you about that project," Miranda said, "when you have a minute."

Bette, looking frightened, said, "I've got to run, Brinks. Catch you later."

When the room was empty, Miranda said, "*Being John Malkovitch.*"

"Huh?"

"*Being John Malkovitch.* The movie. Ever seen it?"

"Yeah. I rented it once. I hated it. Cameron Diaz looked *so bad.* Can you believe how bad she looked? I mean, *Cameron Diaz!*"

"Work with me, Barbie!" said Miranda. "The premise: There's a portal into John Malkovitch's head. That's how the other people get to be John Malkovitch."

"I get what you're saying. But I don't think there's a portal. It happens when I'm asleep. I wish there were a portal, though, so I could stay away from it."

Miranda sighed. "Well, just taking a stab." Then she started giggling. "A stab. Get it?"

"I get it. But that doesn't make it funny."

"Lighten up, Barbie. You know, you're a lot more fun than I imagined. You amuse me."

"Stop calling me Barbie!"

"I can't help it."

"Fine. Then if I'm Barbie, you're . . . I don't know. What are you?"

Miranda nodded her head. "Exactly. That's the look I'm going for. Thank you, Barbie! Hey, what period do you see Matt?"

"Fourth, in physics."

"Ask him again about comingled atoms or whatever. It can't hurt to explore all the possibilities."

"Matt's still not talking to me."

"He will be by fourth period. I've got second with him. I'll talk to him. You just worry about getting him to explain the physics stuff to you. Today. And don't take no for an answer."

Brinkley smiled.

"And don't look so confident," Miranda said. "I know you're not used to hearing the word 'no' from guys, but let's just hope that by fourth period, you've still got your own eyelashes to bat at him."

chapter twenty-five

"Hey, Brinkley Brinkerson."

Obviously, Miranda had done her job well.

"So, you're talking to me again?"

"I was never not talking to you," Matt said.

"Yes, you were. You were *so* not talking to me!"

"No, I wasn't. That would imply that I was sulking. Guys don't sulk. That's strictly for chicks."

Someone should tell Tristan, Brinkley thought. As of that morning, he was still pouting about her refusal to go parking.

"I'm sorry I missed our appointment the other day, Matt. It's just that—"

"No sweat. Miranda told me you drove her to work. She said she was in a panic one day when her ride didn't show up, and you offered her a ride. I think Miranda has a rough time at home. She could use a friend. That was really nice of you to do that."

"You sound surprised," she said.

"No, not really. I mean, other people might be surprised, but I'm not."

"But, you can't tell anyone," she said. "It would damage my rep."

"Yeah, we can't have everyone knowing how nice you really are. Consider it in the vault."

Ms. Ouderkirk came by the lab table, carrying a container of water for the day's experiment on surface tension. She accidentally bumped the edge and lost her grip on the container, spilling water and soaking Brinkley and Matt's books as well as the surrounding area. "Oh, I'm so sorry!" said Ms. Ouderkirk. "Brinkley, would you mind running to the janitor's closet and getting a mop and some paper towels?"

"No problem."

Like most high school students when given a hall pass, Brinkley felt that it was not only her right but her duty to loiter as long as possible. Though the janitor's closet was only the next hall over, Brinkley noticed the lights weren't on in the theater. *Must be Ellis's prep period,* she thought. She decided to investigate the empty auditorium. After all, her family had paid for it.

The large room was pitch black except for the exit signs on either side, which glowed like green cat's-eyes. Brinkley ran her hand along the painted cement-block wall in the back and switched on the lights with a loud click. She walked slowly down the left aisle, taking in the emptiness of so many chairs, their seats all flipped up. Just past the front row, she looked down into the orchestra pit. There was nothing but a few extension cords and a candy bar wrapper. She walked around the railing, up the stage steps. For a while, she stood in the center, imagining all the people who would be looking at her during the school play. She smiled and hugged her arms around herself at the pleasant warmth of the thought.

She decided to poke around backstage. She touched the heavy curtains and thick ropes, peered up at the lights with all the different gels over the bulbs. She stretched and let out a protracted yawn.

The stillness of the empty theater made her aware of how incredibly sleepy she was. And why wouldn't she feel sleepy? She'd had a long couple of weeks, to say the least. Jumps were bound to take a toll on a person.

Tucked away in a corner, near some other props and scenery for the upcoming play, stood a vintage-looking smoky blue sofa. A large box sat on top of it, filled with what looked like some sort of lighting equipment. When Brinkley picked up the box to move it, she found the task easier than she'd anticipated. As if she were stronger. She sat down on the sofa. She knew that more than enough time had passed for her to have retrieved the mop from the janitor's closet and returned to physics, but her fatigue felt like a weight on her, and she couldn't resist lying down, just for a minute.

"Honey, wake up," said a woman's voice. Brinkley felt a surge of adrenaline. How could she have fallen asleep? Ms. Ouderkirk was going to flip. What time was it? How long had she been out?

But the blue sofa wasn't underneath her. She was sitting upright in a chair, at a desk.

In the school office.

"Mr. Russell needs you to go mop up a spill in the science lab," said Mrs. Ingram, the school secretary. Brinkley just stared at her. "Come on, Ivy. Chop, chop!" *Ivy?* Ivy Ingram?

Sophomore Ivy Ingram had been A-list at Story High since, well, since forever. Her dad was a magazine publisher, and not only had they had a seriously nice house in Brinkley's neighborhood, Ivy had always had the coolest clothes of any girl at school, next to Brinkley. But sometime last year, Ivy had completely fallen off the radar. Her family had moved into a different, less chichi neighborhood. Mrs. Ingram had told Brinkley's mom that they'd just felt simply *lost* in that big house and wanted to simplify. And Mrs. Ingram, who'd never worked and had been part of the same country-club tennis league as Dr. Harper, had become a school secretary a couple of months ago. "I just want to spend as much time as possible with Ivy," Brinkley remembered Mrs. Ingram telling her mom one day at the club. "And Gary and I thought that working at the school would be a great way to know what Ivy is up to and who her friends are. You know, you just can't be too careful these days." Come to think of it, Brinkley hadn't seen the Ingrams at the club since then.

Brinkley hadn't seen much of Ivy at all this year. She'd dropped out of the party scene, and she wasn't dating anyone important . . . or anyone at all, as far as Brinkley knew. She hadn't noticed Ivy wearing anything particularly interesting in some time. In fact, she hadn't noticed Ivy, *period,* this year.

"Don't worry. If any of the other kids ask, just laugh it off and say they couldn't find anyone else, so they made you do it since you're the office assistant this period. No one will know."

No one will know *what?*

What was a former It Girl like Ivy Ingram doing on mop duty?

chapter twenty-six

There were only twenty minutes left before Brinkley's physics class ended. She collected herself and went into the bathroom to look in the mirror. Ivy was one of those girls who was neither pretty nor unpretty, but could be attractive with the right hair, makeup, and clothes. Her figure was slim but athletic, probably from being the star player on the school volleyball team. She had rock-hard triceps, which explained why Brinkley had moved that heavy box so easily. Being Ivy wasn't as much of a change as it had been being Miranda, Carly, or Jae. While it wasn't ideal to be in someone else's body, Brinkley was almost getting used to it, and besides, how bad could it be to be Ivy Ingram? She was pretty normal.

She went to retrieve the mop from the janitor's closet but couldn't find it anywhere. The closet was a narrow room only about six feet long, packed with lemony-smelling cleaners and vomit-absorbing powders. Yuck. Convinced it was gone, Brinkley went back to Ms. Ouderkirk's room, where she found the custodian busily mopping up the water that had been spilled earlier. Ms. Ouderkirk was lecturing, but stopped when she saw Ivy in the doorway. "May I help you?" she asked.

"Oh . . . I work in the office this period," said Brinkley.

"And what can we do for you?"

Obviously, she wasn't needed for mop duty anymore (score!), so

Brinkley had to think fast for a response. "Brinkley Harper had to check out," she said.

"Is she all right?"

"I think she has a virus or something," she said. She glanced at Matt, who had a look of concern on his face.

"That is unfortunate. Thank you."

Not bad, Brinkley, she thought. *You might as well use Ivy to cover for yourself, things being what they are.*

Brinkley went back to the office and gathered Ivy's things before the bell. She needed to check Ivy's schedule to find out where to go next. She sat down at the empty computer and moved the mouse so that the screen saver vanished and the desktop came up. The login said "Office4," but wouldn't allow her access without a password.

"Hey, Mrs. . . . Mom," she said. "I forgot my password."

Mrs. Ingram sighed. "How could you possibly forget your password?"

"You're always saying I'd forget my head if it wasn't attached."

Apparently, Mrs. Ingram was always saying that, because she replied, "It's Hawaii—with @ for the *a*'s and exclamation points for the *i*'s."

Brinkley glanced to the right of the monitor at a photo of the Ingrams at a luau, smiling, wearing leis, and holding cups that looked like pineapples. She typed in "h@w@!!" and the screen unlocked.

Brinkley was delighted to discover that Office4 had access to nearly every interesting file in the school's database. The capital-campaign report indicated who had donated what amounts for the school's new facilities. Bette's family had given the bare minimum of five-hundred dollars to make it into the Donors' Circle, while the

Harpers were in the Benefactors' Circle with Tristan's family. The college counselor's file listed all juniors' and seniors' SAT scores and where they'd been offered early admission or scholarships. *HA!* she thought, *I knew Angela Weber was lying about admission to Princeton!* Angela's verbal scores on the SAT didn't exactly suck, but they weren't going to get her in. And after all that insufferable talk about how Angela had decided that Princeton "just didn't feel like the right choice" for her after all. Wait until she told Bette about *this.*

Brinkley wanted to look at more—there was even a list of disciplinary referrals dating back to 2007!—but the bell rang. Quickly, she opened up the class-schedules file and printed out Ivy's.

There were only three more periods left before the day was over, and Ivy at least spoke English, so Brinkley was able to slip by in her classes without too much trouble, other than where-do-I-sit? type issues.

Ivy had a learner's permit in her wallet, so she couldn't have driven alone. That meant Brinkley didn't have to concern herself with finding Ivy's car in the parking lot after school. She probably rode with her mom. Brinkley went up to the office and sat down at the desk again. Mrs. Ingram was on the phone, so she decided she'd make use of the time to go through those confidential files on the computer again. This whole jumping thing could be useful.

"Ivy, what are you doing?" Mrs. Ingram asked.

"Just waiting for you," Brinkley said.

"You're supposed to be in the lunchroom."

"I'm supposed to be in the lunchroom," Brinkley repeated slowly.

"I know you don't like it, honey, but it's the only way. We've been over this. We all have to work to stay afloat. Now hurry before they call up here looking for you."

Had Ivy Ingram's dad lost his job?

Well, it made sense. A ton of magazines had folded when the recession hit. Come to think of it, it had been a while since she'd seen that yachting magazine lying on her family's coffee table. Wasn't that the one Ivy's dad had owned? And wasn't it around the height of the recession that Ivy had stopped dressing so cute and started avoiding the in-crowd? When Brinkley put all the pieces together, it was so obvious, she couldn't believe she hadn't seen it before. There had been no "simplifying." The Ingrams had to sell their house and give up their country-club membership.

This was just the kind of dirt Brinkley would have been dying to dish to Bette a few days ago. But now she thought of how the rumor about Miranda had spread so quickly and how this information about Ivy would make the rounds equally fast, only Ivy wouldn't enjoy it the way Miranda had. She thought of the whispers and condescending stares—certainly none of that would be fun for Ivy.

The thought of embarrassing Ivy caused Brinkley to feel something unfamiliar: a twinge of conscience.

chapter twenty-seven

*B*rinkley stood just inside the kitchen area, where the green melamine trays lay stacked next to the silverware bins. The steel trays of food had been removed, and the hot water underneath steamed. Two women worked in the kitchen. One was scrubbing down empty food containers in the sink, soaking them with hot water from a large spray nozzle. The other was crumbling leftover hamburger into a large vat.

"You waiting for an engraved invitation?" the one with the hamburger meat asked.

"Oh," said Brinkley. "No. I . . . I just didn't know what you wanted me to do."

"The usual," she said. "Start by wiping down the sneeze guards."

It didn't take Brinkley long to figure out what the woman meant. Though she had never heard nor contemplated the name of the clear plastic roofs over the food dishes, the name was disgustingly apt and descriptive.

She looked around until she found a spray bottle and a rag—a damp, cold, stained rag—and began cleaning the sneeze guards. When she finished, the hamburger woman motioned for her to come into the kitchen proper, behind the food line. As Brinkley obeyed, she received a shrill, *"Eh-eh-eh!"* from the cook.

"What?" Brinkley said.

"Aren't you forgetting something?"

"Permission to enter the kitchen area, sir?"

"Very funny," said the woman. "Get your hairnet on."

Hairnet?

Oh, no no no no no. There is only so much humiliation I am willing to tolerate! Brinkley thought. *Ivy Ingram can just lose her stupid little job for all I care.* "You know what? I'm thinking, no hairnet today. Is that cool with you?" The woman, still stone-faced, said nothing. "Good. Then we understand each other."

The woman took off her clear plastic gloves, marched past Brinkley, and picked up a hairnet, which she unceremoniously snapped onto Brinkley's (Ivy's) head without a word.

Brinkley was accustomed to being dismissive of people like the cook: Tallulah, her parents' office staff, waiters, tutors . . . she'd even considered her teachers the hired help. But something about this woman, this situation, was kind of scary. Brinkley doubted she'd have the courage to cross her, even in her own body. So she tucked her hair into the hairnet and awaited further instructions.

"Wash up and put on your gloves," said the cook.

Brinkley went to the sink, washed, and pulled a pair of the clear gloves from a nearby dispenser.

"Open those cans and put them in here."

Brinkley picked up a can of chili the size of one of the geranium planters on her front porch. She had no idea what to do with it.

"Did you forget where the can opener is?" the cook asked. She scoffed and pointed at an electrical device. Brinkley gingerly approached it and tried to maneuver the lip of the giant can into a groove on the device. She caught her breath when the machine grabbed hold of the can and began spinning it around with a whirring sound. When it was finished, Brinkley took the open can to the cook.

"Dump it in there," she said. Brinkley turned her face away and held the can at arm's length as the chili exited the can with a *squoosh*. "Well, scrape the can!" the cook ordered.

Brinkley looked around. "Where's the spoon?"

"Spoon?" the cook replied. "Scrape it!" She mimed a C-shape with her plastic-coated hand until Brinkley realized that she was supposed to put her own hand inside the can. "Come on, I don't have all day!" the cook yelled. Even though Brinkley's skin wasn't in direct contact with the cold chili, she winced at the sensation of the lumpy substance against her hand. The cook continued crumbling meat into the vat.

"Are those the hamburgers from today's lunch?" Brinkley asked.

"Yeah. What about it?"

"Nothing," said Brinkley, swearing to herself that she would never, ever eat lunchroom food again, no matter what. She and her classmates had always thought that lunchroom meals were kind of gross, but now that she had been behind the scenes, she'd starve before she'd touch anything from this kitchen.

After Brinkley had scooped all the chili, the cook said, "You're completely useless in here today. Take off your gloves and get out of here."

I'm free! Brinkley thought. But just when she'd removed the hairnet and gloves and could almost taste her liberation, the cook handed her a putty knife. "What am I supposed to do with this?" Brinkley said.

"Gum duty."

"What's gum . . ."

Before she could finish her question, Brinkley realized exactly what gum duty meant.

The only way for Brinkley to scrape the gum off was to crawl underneath the lunchroom tables, sit on the cold, hard floor, and get to work with the putty knife.

Ivy Ingram was not worth this. But when Brinkley thought about sneaking away, the hamburger lady eyed her menacingly from the kitchen.

Why is this happening to me? Brinkley thought. *I don't deserve this!*

But even Brinkley knew that, no matter how comforting it might be to wallow in self-pity, to say she didn't deserve this fate wouldn't be entirely true. Or maybe not even mostly true. If she were being punished, she had it coming. And not just the gum-duty part—though the poetic justice of the situation did not escape her.

She sat down and began scraping. At first, the task was nauseating. Some of the gums still retained a slight minty or fruity scent. *I will never, ever put my gum under the desk again,* she thought. *In fact, I will never chew gum again, period.* But as time went on, she found a strange satisfaction in seeing the immediate results of her labor. She even felt a fleeting glee when a piece of gum came off in a single hard chunk instead of a sticky glob.

"Having fun?" the cook asked. She was clutching a purse and wearing an overcoat. She had removed her hairnet.

"Right."

"It's time to go."

"Oh," Brinkley said. "All right." It hadn't occurred to her that she had a specific time frame in which to work. Ivy would have to finish the rest of the tables another day, when Brinkley was back to being herself. Because she *would* be back to herself soon, of course. None of the jumps had lasted for more than a few hours.

Brinkley returned her putty knife, washed up, and went to meet Ivy's mother back at the school office. On the way, she passed the auditorium, where play practice was still in session. She'd missed another rehearsal.

"Mr. Ellis," she said.

"Yes?" The actors on stage fell silent as everyone turned to look at Ivy.

"Brinkley Harper's physician called the office and asked that she be excused from all activities today due to an illness."

"All right," said Mr. Ellis. "Thank you."

Wasn't he even going to ask what was wrong with her? Didn't he care? And the practice seemed to be going on just fine without her. Shouldn't it have been difficult to work around her absence? She was, after all, the star.

Emma was onstage reading lines with the girl who played Laura's mother. Brinkley watched for a few minutes. Mr. Ellis was beaming. When the scene was over, he said, "Emma, that was fantastic. You really get Tennessee Williams and his incredible compassion for his characters. You bring a real tenderness to the role."

No one seemed to notice when Ivy Ingram left the auditorium.

"I don't know about you, but I'm beat," said Mrs. Ingram when Brinkley walked into the office. She grabbed her keys, and the two of them went to collect Ivy's six-year-old identical twin brothers, Taylor and Tyler, from their after-school program. On the way home, the boys sang thirty-nine repetitions of a song they'd invented called "Spiderman and His Panties," laughing hysterically all the while. Brinkley's head (or, more properly, Ivy's) was ready to explode.

"Wouldn't it be quicker and easier to just bore a screwdriver into your temples?" she asked Mrs. Ingram.

"Come on, Ivy," said Mrs. Ingram. "I didn't think their little games even registered on your radar anymore. Besides, at least they're not arguing." She handed Brinkley a tissue from the console. "Can you wipe Tyler's nose?"

Brinkley took the tissue and stared at Mrs. Ingram. Wiping some kid's snot was worse than scraping gum. "Here, Tyler. Wipe your nose," Brinkley said, handing the tissue back in the general direction of the boys. A piercing whine escaped one of the twins.

"No! No! No! No! No!"

"Ivy, just forget it. It can wait until we get home," Mrs. Ingram said.

Brinkley had no idea where the Ingrams were living these days or even what housing actually cost, but when they drove to a less desirable part of town, Brinkley remembered hearing something once about how the three most important aspects of real estate were location, location, and location. The Ingrams had moved to Oak Manor, a neighborhood that had been upscale about thirty years ago. The homes were large and well made, mostly painted brick, but had lost their resale value over the years as more and more apartments, convenience stores, and fast-food restaurants had begun popping up in the vicinity. The trendy had moved north of town and built McMansions with well-maintained pools and underground utilities. Oak Manor had become passé.

From the time they hit the front door that afternoon, the Ingram household was a madhouse. Mrs. Ingram instructed Brinkley to load the dishwasher while she checked on the pot roast. "Thank goodness for the crock pot!" she said as she lifted the lid and the aroma filled the kitchen. Brinkley, without plastic gloves this time, had to rinse cookie-shaped cereal out of bowls and place them in the dishwasher. She'd never actually put anything in a dishwasher before; that was why they had Tallulah.

"Why are you putting the cereal bowls on the bottom rack?" Mrs. Ingram asked. "Place the silverware end up in the basket, honey. You know they'll never get clean the other way." Apparently, families who did this sort of thing for themselves had predetermined little arrangements that they followed.

"Can you make Taylor and Tyler's dinner for me?" Mrs. Ingram asked.

"What do you mean?" asked Brinkley. They didn't still eat baby food or something, did they? "Can't they eat the stuff in the crock pot?" That stuff smelled kind of good, actually. It wasn't Tallulah's veal cutlets, but it made her mouth water nonetheless.

"Those two picky boys eat pot roast? You know Taylor and Tyler better than that!" Mrs. Ingram had no idea how ironic her statement was. She handed Brinkley a box of fish sticks, a can of peaches, and a tube of crescent rolls. Brinkley was in business: The fish sticks box had directions on the back. The crescent rolls were less of a success, ending up looking more like small speed bumps than actual crescents, but Brinkley figured they weren't bad for her first try.

Ivy's dad came home around six o'clock from his new job, which, Brinkley was able to deduce, had something to do with editing brochures for a medical or pharmaceutical company. Definitely a big step down from publishing a yachting magazine. But Mr. Ingram didn't complain. As soon as he walked through the door, he seemed to shut out the rest of the world, dropping his satchel and immediately wrestling with the twins. When Mr. Ingram made his way into the kitchen, with one twin hanging onto each leg, he kissed

Mrs. Ingram on the cheek and hugged his daughter. It felt weird to Brinkley, especially when he loudly zerberted the back of her neck, but at the same time, it made her feel she was missing something. Her own dad never behaved in this way. While Brinkley's father was serious and distracted, Mr. Ingram was goofy and present.

The Ingram family actually sat down to dinner together, and each was expected to share something about his or her day. Brinkley couldn't remember the last time both of her parents had been home for dinner. When they were, they usually had the television on so they could watch the stock market report while they ate.

"What was your high today, Tyler?" Mr. Ingram asked.

"I got a Caught-Being-Good sticker today for turning in a pencil to the Lost and Found!" he announced.

"That's awesome!" Mr. Ingram said. "What about you, Taylor?"

Taylor had to think before answering, "I made a robot!"

Mrs. Ingram said, "A robot! When do you get to bring it home so we can see it?"

Taylor wasn't sure, but the whole family seemed eager to get a glimpse, so Taylor described his can robot in detail.

"Ivy, how about you?" asked Mr. Ingram.

"Huh?"

"Your high?" said Ivy's dad. He grinned. "What was the very best part of your day?"

"Oh," Brinkley said. What was the best part of Ivy's day? The gum scraping? The chili making? The hairnet? The family waited for her response. Even the twins were quiet.

Finally, Brinkley replied. "The best part of my day," she said, "is right now."

chapter twenty-eight

*I*t didn't surprise Brinkley in the least that, after going to bed as Ivy Ingram, she woke up in her own bed as Brinkley Harper.

Whatever this phenomenon was, each jump seemed to be temporary. Brinkley wondered if she were the only person ever to experience it. Maybe lots of people had this happen to them, but like her, they were afraid to tell anyone. Maybe, whenever someone was absent from school, they weren't really sick but just inhabiting someone else's body. It would certainly explain why people sometimes acted so weird.

As Brinkley lay in bed, pondering her time as Ivy, a quiet rage overtook her. It wasn't fair that the Ingrams had family dinners together while she ate alone and her parents lived it up in Bora-Bora.

This jumping business had almost made her go soft, but she wouldn't let that happen again. From now on, Brinkley would remember that her first priority was to herself, no matter whose body she was in.

Irirangi had arranged for more morning sessions to accommodate Brinkley's afternoon play practices (which, one of these days, she was really going to have to start showing up for). She thought of how Irirangi had acted at their last session, all that stuff about how much her pants cost. Brinkley decided she'd been too easy on Irirangi and she wouldn't make that mistake today. She'd have to show her who was boss.

"So what's today's word?" Brinkley asked when she sat down in her chair in Irirangi's office.

"I don't know what you mean," said Irirangi.

"You know, our little theme for the day. What's our topic?"

"You're angry today."

"So what if I am?"

"Would you like to tell me what you're so angry about, or would you prefer to continue misdirecting your anger toward me?"

"Who says I'm angry?"

"Aren't you?"

"Maybe I am."

"What do you think is causing you to feel angry?"

"I don't know. A lot of things! Like, why do I have to come to these stupid counseling sessions when other people just get to do what they want?"

"What are other people doing that you would like to be doing right now?"

"Nothing special—just living normal lives."

"And what do normal people do that you aren't doing?"

Brinkley huffed. "Just average stuff."

"Such as?"

"I don't know! Eating pot roast, talking about their day."

"With whom?"

Brinkley clenched her teeth and felt her face get hot. "With their families, maybe." Irirangi pushed a box of tissues closer to Brinkley. "What, you think I'm going to cry?" Brinkley said, just before the first tear rolled down her cheek.

"It's fine if you do," Irirangi said. "Sometimes it helps." She waited a moment before continuing. "Would it make you happy to eat pot roast and talk about your day with your family, Brinkley?"

"It might," Brinkley said. "But it's not going to happen. My parents are in Bora-Bora. They don't even call. But who cares, because they're going to bring me back something 'fabulous.' That fixes everything, doesn't it?"

"So it's your parents you're angry with."

Brinkley rubbed her face hard. "I'm not talking to you about my parents. Can't we just get on with whatever little regularly scheduled kumbayah you've cooked up?"

Irirangi smiled. "I'm glad to know you appreciate my preparedness for our sessions. Actually, I would like to address a particular issue today. One that, given the reason for your referral, I believe will be of great value to us. I'd like to talk about compassion. We've talked before about how you see others and how you see yourself. And that lays the groundwork for today. Brinkley, why don't you tell me what compassion means to you?"

"Who cares?" Brinkley replied. "This is beyond lame."

"Why? What's wrong with being kind to someone?"

"Nothing. It's the best. It's great. Can I go now?"

"Let me ask a different question. Has anyone ever been compassionate towards you?"

"Of course."

"Give me an example."

Brinkley let out a big sigh. "Let's see. . . . A couple of years ago, when I had the stomach flu, Tallulah took care of me."

"And who is Tallulah?"

"Our housekeeper."

"And?"

"And she was really nice. She stayed with me all night long because my parents were both working late. I was thirsty, but I couldn't keep down even a sip of water. So she fed me ice chips. And the next day when I finally felt like I could eat, she brought me some crackers. But they were those round, buttery kind, and I couldn't eat them. I was too sick to eat anything that rich. So she went out and bought me Saltines."

Irirangi nodded. "And why do you think Tallulah was so kind to you?"

Brinkley laughed halfheartedly. "It's kind of her job."

"But isn't what you described a bit over and above?"

"Maybe." Brinkley thought a minute. "Once, when I was about six, I overheard Tallulah talking to another grown-up at the park. I think it was somebody's mom, trying to get her to come and work for them. She wouldn't do it. She told the lady, 'The child needs me.' I never said anything about it to her or to my parents, but I've kind of always thought that she puts up with my family because of me. Like in some way, she thinks of me as her own kid."

"As though she's assumed the role for an absent parent?"

"I guess." Brinkley reminded herself not to let down her guard again. "But you can't think of it that way. It blurs the boundaries."

"You mean between employer and subordinate," said Irirangi.

"Yeah."

"Do you think you might be afraid of blurring other boundaries, with people besides Tallulah? People who don't work for your family?"

"I don't know what you're talking about," Brinkley said.

"Do you think that maybe you're afraid that if you show kindness to others, you might enter into a situation that could end up hurting you? That maybe you're afraid showing compassion makes you in some way vulnerable?"

Brinkley scoffed. "No . . . I mean . . . I don't even know what you're trying to say. Look, you wanted an example of someone being nice to me, and I gave you one. Tallulah fed me ice chips and gave me some Saltines. It's not like she brought peace to the Middle East or anything. It's really no big deal."

"Maybe not," said Irirangi. "But then, why did you remember it?"

Later that day, at school, Brinkley tried not to dwell on what Irirangi had said about Tallulah. Tallulah had done her job. The Harpers paid her for things like that. The fact that Brinkley remembered it was irrelevant. One always had to acknowledge the quality of service one received—like the time her car's detailing hadn't been up to her standards. People at the Harpers' level had to pay attention to these things to make sure they weren't being taken advantage of. Brinkley had, after all, given Tallulah an extra day off when she'd gotten well. They were even.

But, not thinking about Tallulah after that session was like someone saying, "Don't think about elephants": It was all she could think about. She kept wondering why Tallulah put up with her, why she'd refused an offer for another job all those years ago because she felt Brinkley needed her. She'd always treated Tallulah like a robot. Now she wondered what Tallulah's life was really like, what she did when she wasn't at work, what she really thought of Brinkley. What if Brinkley jumped into Tallulah? Brinkley wondered if these jumps were limited to the students at Story High or if she might end up living a day as Tallulah or even some random person. What if she had to work for and put up with Brinkley Harper day after day? The more she pondered it, the less she thought she'd like it.

There were a lot of things she needed to think about. Like why and how these jumps were happening to her.

At lunch, she passed by Bette, Tristan, and her usual group. "Where are you going, Brinks?" Bette asked.

"I've got to get that Matt guy to help me with something for physics." She stopped off at the freak table and said to Miranda, "Think your rep can handle eating lunch with me?"

"Is that a challenge?" Miranda asked.

Brinkley said, loudly enough for the other Goths to hear, "Yes, I will let you sit with me to discuss your trying out for the cheerleading squad."

"Very funny, Barbie," Miranda said.

They went to Matt's table and asked his friends to make room for them. They seemed surprised, to say the least.

"This is an unexpected honor," Matt said.

"Miranda and I are extremely interested in possibly joining the physics club," Brinkley said.

"You hate physics, Brinkley," he replied. "And Miranda doesn't even take physics."

"All the more reason you should discuss physics with us," Brinkley said, "to encourage us to appreciate the subject."

"OK. What do you want to talk about?"

Brinkley pretended to think. "Oh, why don't you tell Miranda about that Einstein thing, with the quantum tangles."

Matt grinned. "Quantum entanglement? You really dig that, don't you?"

"It's less boring than the other stuff," Brinkley said.

"I looked up some stuff on it, but it's pretty complicated. All I really know is that they use the theory for computers. Qubits existing simultaneously in more than one state."

"What's a qubit?" Miranda asked.

"A unit of quantum information," Matt said.

"That clears up everything," Brinkley said.

"I told you, it's hard stuff. Polarizing beam splitters, things way over my head."

"Can it apply to people?" Miranda asked.

"What? People existing in two places at once?" asked Matt. "No, that's absurd. There's no way to apply classical statistics to large-scale matter. Like I told Brinkley, it's all science fiction when you apply it to people."

"Thanks, Matt. That was really interesting," Brinkley said. She gathered her lunch and took Miranda aside. "There's no scientific explanation for this. It's not natural."

"I agree," Miranda said. "So if it's not natural, you know what that means, don't you?"

"What?"

"It's supernatural."

chapter twenty-nine

To distract herself from the possibility that supernatural forces were at work in her life, Brinkley spent the rest of the lunch period learning her lines for the play. She was pleased with her dedication, though a little disappointed when she finally realized that Laura Wingfield was a ginormous bag o' crazy who talked about glass animals as though they were real. But whatever. She'd still be onstage a long time.

That afternoon, Brinkley had a better rehearsal than before. Uncharacteristically absorbed in the role of Laura Wingfield, she didn't notice when Emma Paulis retired to the dressing room to nurse a headache.

Right about the time the "gentleman caller" broke the horn off Laura Wingfield's glass unicorn, Brinkley began to feel lightheaded. She stared at the actor playing Jim and steadied herself against the couch.

"Brinkley, are you all right?" asked Mr. Ellis.

"Yeah," she replied. "I just haven't eaten much today." That was true. After talking with Matt and Miranda, she'd studied her lines during lunch and barely touched a bite.

"Why don't you take a break?" Mr. Ellis said. "Maybe take five and have a snack? There's a vending machine in the teacher's lounge. Do you need some change?"

"No thanks—I have some. Be back in a sec."

As soon as Brinkley was through the auditorium doors, Miranda was right behind her. "You OK?"

"I'm fine," Brinkley said. "It's just my blood sugar."

"You sure about that?"

"Totally. Don't worry."

"Copacetic, then. But if you're wrong, just come and find me. You know where I'll be," she said, waving her paintbrush.

In the lounge, Brinkley bought a Diet Sprite and a pack of crackers with fake cheese. She took a few sips of the drink and sat down to rest until her blood sugar got back to normal.

"You feeling better?" said the actress who played Laura Wingfield's mother. Jenna was so right for the part: All hips and thighs and frump, even at sixteen. She was adjusting her hair in the mirror and had her back to Brinkley. "Ellis ended practice early since you're sick and the monster bailed. She totally skipped out without a word. What a shocker."

What monster? Brinkley wondered.

When Brinkley didn't respond, Jenna said, "Wake up, sleepyhead! Don't forget that we've got Dave's party tonight!"

Brinkley was now awake enough to realize she wasn't in the teacher's lounge but in the backstage dressing room. She didn't know any Dave, and she wouldn't be caught dead at a party with Jenna.

Uh-oh.

Brinkley got up from the bench she'd been lying on and caught a glimpse of herself in the mirror in front of Jenna. She recognized the sensible bobbed hair and the short, slight form drowning in an oversized sweater.

She started giggling. Of all people . . .

"Emma, what's so funny?" Jenna said.

That made Brinkley laugh all the more.

"Seriously, what is up with you?"

"I'm . . ." Brinkley laughed again. "I'm . . ." She could barely get the words out. "I'm Emma Paulis, the nicest girl in school!"

Jenna laughed a little bit too, probably because she didn't know what else to do. "Yeah, Emma," she said. "You are the nicest person in school. Probably in the whole world!"

"I probably am!" she replied, still giggling.

"OK," said Jenna, "I don't see what's so hilarious, but whatever. Look, we don't have much time before the party."

"Party?" Brinkley said, calming down and wiping her eyes with a tissue from the dressing table.

"Yeah—Dave's party. You've been talking about it for weeks."

"Right," Brinkley said. "Partying with Dave tonight. Can't wait! Wild Man Dave!"

Jenna chuckled. "Do you need me to give you a lift?"

"Actually, yes. That would be great," she said. "But I have to do one thing first. Can you wait for me out in front of the school?"

"Sure, Emma. No prob."

Brinkley gathered her own backpack and located her keys.

"Isn't that Brinkley's stuff?" asked Jenna.

"Yeah, she asked me to pick it up for her."

"You really are the nicest person in the world," Jenna said, rolling her eyes.

Brinkley went to find Miranda, who was waiting outside for Brinkley to drive her to work. "What's shakin'?" Brinkley asked.

"Hi, Emma," Miranda said absently. "What are you up to?"

"I dunno. . . . Got any weed?" Brinkley burst into another fit of giggling.

Miranda looked puzzled. "I beg your pardon?"

"Oh, come on, Goth Girl. Can't you help a goody two-shoes score a doobie?"

Miranda scowled. "Oh, no! Brinkley?" Brinkley nodded, still laughing. "That's not funny!" Miranda half whispered, half hissed. "For a minute there, I thought Emma Paulis was trying to take a walk on the wild side."

"Look, obviously, I can't drive you to work today, so take my car," Brinkley said, handing her the keys. "And while you're at it, throw my backpack in there so I can find it tomorrow. Drive yourself to work or wherever. I've got good insurance, so don't sweat it. Just pick me up tomorrow for school, OK?"

"Your car? Brinkley, are you sure?"

"Hey, I promised you a ride to work, didn't I?"

"Yeah, but what about you? Are you going to be OK?"

Brinkley grinned. "Don't worry about me. Everything is . . . what's your word? Copacetic. Emma Paulis is going to a party tonight! Can you imagine?"

"So what? What's that got to do with you?"

"Don't you realize how fun this could be?"

"Do you really think a party that Emma's going to could be that much fun for you? I mean, Emma doesn't strike me as the party-animal type. Probably not your kind of scene."

"Look, I don't know why any of this is happening to me, but it's nothing permanent. I go to sleep, I wake up as somebody else. Then I go back to sleep and wake up as myself. Why? Who knows? But I don't see any reason I can't have a little fun with it."

"What kind of fun did you have in mind?"

"Come *on*, Miranda! Emma Paulis, the world's squarest square. She's so square, she's practically . . . a cube!"

"And your point is?"

"Emma Paulis is going to a party tonight. And Emma Paulis, for once in her miserable life, is going to have some fun!"

"Brinkley, what are you going to do to her?"

"Nothing! Just what I said. Have a little fun!"

"I don't like this, Brinkley. It's not right. You shouldn't mess around with Emma's life just because you've taken over her body. She doesn't deserve it."

"Take it easy. This is as much for Emma's benefit as mine."

"No, it's not. You're being selfish and you know it."

"I knew I should have confided in Bette about this! What was I thinking, trusting you? You know what? Just forget the whole thing! I've got this figured out now and I don't need your help. You are absolutely no fun. No wonder you don't have any friends."

"Get bent!" Miranda yelled. "You're on your own!"

"Fine!" Brinkley yelled back. "Then you can't take my car!"

"Wanna bet?"

"I'll call the cops and report it stolen!" Brinkley called after her as Miranda began to walk away.

Miranda turned around. "You do that," she said. "Of course, they'll ask you to file a police report and show them your ID, which might be kind of difficult since you aren't in your own body."

Brinkley fumed. "You'd better hope you get to my house tomorrow morning early, because I'll be back to normal, and if you're not there, I won't have any trouble calling the cops then!"

Miranda kept walking, which infuriated Brinkley all the more. She'd decided a long time ago that it was far better to be hated than ignored.

"There you are, Emma!" Jenna said. "Ready to go?"

"Oh, I'm ready," she said. "I am so ready. Should we swing by my place first so I can get changed?"

Jenna looked at her watch. "I don't think we have time for that. The party starts in less than an hour."

Less than an hour? That was five o'clock What kind of party started before dark? "I guess I could hurry," Brinkley said. "I can't really wear this to a party."

"Sure you can, Emma," Jenna said. "You look great. Besides, I don't think we could make it out to your house in time. We have to stop off at my house to pick up the supplies."

Of course! Brinkley thought. *Supplies!*

"You've got the supplies at your house?"

"Yeah. I meant to bring them to school with me, but I forgot."

What amateurs. Everyone knew you couldn't bring your party supplies to school, not unless you *wanted* to get busted.

"Were you able to score a keg or did you have to get cans?"

Jenna nudged Emma. "Silly! Listen, you're welcome to freshen up at my house if you want while I put stuff in the trunk."

"All right," Brinkley said. It was better than nothing.

When they arrived at Jenna's house, Brinkley found Jenna's bathroom and began trying to do something about Emma's ridiculous forty-year-old-bank-teller hair. Luckily, Jenna's flat iron heated up pretty quickly, and Brinkley was able to transform Emma's boingy *don't* into a sleek, poker-straight *do* teased in the back. Then she drew on some black eyeliner to create a kittenish Angelina Jolie look.

She pouted in the mirror, more or less satisfied. But there was still the matter of the clothes. If the sweater had been only slightly longer, she might've been able to stretch it into a dress, but as it was, there was nothing that could be done.

Unless she borrowed something of Jenna's.

Jenna's closet connected to the bathroom. There wasn't much to choose from, but Brinkley found a black-and-white-striped knit dress, which, when folded, transformed into a miniskirt. It didn't look half bad with the Mary Janes Emma was already wearing. She topped it with a graphic-print tee that she found wedged in the back, along with some other clothes that looked too small for Jenna. The T-shirt was too small for Emma, too, which made it supertight and gave the outfit some sexiness. Emma's body wasn't half bad, but who would've ever known it, the way she hid under those baggy clothes?

Brinkley was admiring her handiwork in the full-length mirror on the closet door when Jenna poked her head in and asked, "Emma, you ready to . . . go?" She stared a moment before asking, "What did you do?"

"You like it?" Brinkley asked. She was a little thrown by the way Jenna continued to stare as though she'd just gazed upon Medusa. "Come on. . . . It's not that drastic."

"Yes, it is," Jenna said. "It's very drastic."

"Chill. We're going to a party, right? You've got to ramp it up a little bit." Brinkley worried that maybe she'd gone too far. She was supposed to be Emma, after all. She decided to throw in a mention of the guy whose party it was, to keep Jenna from getting suspicious.

"Trust me. The guys will love it. Dave's eyes will pop out of his head."

"Probably," said Jenna. "Or maybe his teeth will pop out of his mouth."

Brinkley laughed at Jenna's random remark. "Yeah, whatever," she said. "I'm ready to party. Let's go!"

chapter thirty

*W*here are we going?" Brinkley asked as Jenna drove down some back streets on the outskirts of town.

"Dave's party."

Cool, Brinkley thought. *This Dave guy must have some party house out in the middle of nowhere.*

Some college frats rented old junk houses just for ragers so they wouldn't lose their charters by having wild goings-on at their campus residences. Maybe the geeks paid dues to some sort of geek society and rented party houses, too.

They pulled up to a large old house that reminded Brinkley of the plantation home in *Jezebel*. She'd always loved that red dress Bette Davis's character had worn to the ball. But, though there were several cars out front, there was no way a house this grand could be a party house. Maybe somebody's parents were out of town. *Where are we?* Brinkley wondered.

She looked past a row of holly bushes and saw a brick sign illuminated by a single spotlight on the lawn. In black metal letters, it said WHISPERING PINES RETIREMENT COMMUNITY.

"Jenna," Brinkley said. "Exactly how old would you say Dave is?"

"Hmmm . . . he said he was nineteen when he joined the Marines, and he was at Iwo Jima in 1945, so I guess we're talking . . . somewhere around ninetyish?"

Oh, no, Brinkley thought as she tugged at her T-shirt, trying to stretch it a little bigger.

"Help me carry in the supplies," Jenna said. They got out of the car and popped the trunk. Jenna handed Brinkley rolls of crepe paper; a big, rolled-up banner; and bags of balloons. She wheeled in a small helium tank. "Let's not get our tank confused with theirs," she joked.

When they walked inside, an attendant smiled warmly at them. "Welcome! The other kids are setting up in the dining hall." Then she looked Brinkley up and down, perplexed. "Go on in, I guess."

Several geeks from school were already there, setting cookies and a big cake that said HAPPY BIRTHDAY DAVE on a table. A guy in a pointy party hat was crouched down with his back to Brinkley and Jenna, pouring ice from a bag into a red cooler. He turned around, and Brinkley caught her breath.

"Hey, Emma, Jenna. What's up?"

"Matt!" said Brinkley.

He smiled. "Yeah. . . . Who were you expecting?"

"I just . . . you're here . . . at this party . . . for this old guy," Brinkley said. "That's so nice."

"Well, you're here, too, Emma," said Matt. "I guess we're both nice!"

Brinkley felt a twinge of shame.

"You look kind of . . . different," Matt said.

Now Brinkley's twinge of shame grew to a full-blown blush of regret.

"I didn't mean to embarrass you," Matt said. "You look great." But Brinkley could tell that Matt was just being polite. What Emma looked like was not at all great given the occasion. It was improper and inappropriate—and entirely Brinkley's fault. Fashion was all about the occasion. She thought again about *Jezebel* and the red dress she'd loved so much from it. Bette Davis's character had worn it out of spite, to shock and offend polite society, when she was supposed to have worn a virginal white gown like all the other young belles. And the plan had backfired on Bette Davis, just like Brinkley's plan was backfiring on her now. She wanted more than anything to get out of there. She shouldn't have done this to Emma. Emma had never done anything to her, or to anyone else, probably, and Brinkley had embarrassed her with this ridiculous getup.

"Matt," she said. "Did you drive here?"

"Yeah."

"Can you take me home?"

"What? What are you talking about, Emma? The party hasn't even started yet. Dave is going to be so excited."

"Can't we just go somewhere else? Just the two of us?" Brinkley hadn't realized it, but she'd put her hand on Matt's arm and had moved closer to him. A little too close. Her need to get out of there, her need for Matt to rescue her, had overcome her. She'd forgotten that he thought she was Emma. Or that she was Emma. Or whatever.

Matt looked uncomfortable. He backed away from Emma, but tried to make it look natural. "You know . . . I think we'd probably just better hang out here. Dave's party and all."

"Matt, I didn't mean . . ." Brinkley began. "It's just that, I don't want to be here right now, and then I saw you, and you're so . . . you're so good, Matt. . . . I just would much rather be somewhere else, with you, where I can feel like myself for a little while, and—"

"Emma," Matt said, "look. I appreciate . . . this. What you're saying. And I think you're a really sweet girl, and I've always thought a lot of you. But I just don't feel that way about you."

Brinkley could think of nothing to say.

"It's not you, not at all," Matt said. "I mean, you're a cute girl and everybody likes you a lot. You're great! It's just that I . . . well, I'm kind of interested in someone else."

"Who?" It was a rude question, far too probing. But Brinkley had never thought of Matt in any context outside of his relationship to her. It was kind of like seeing your teacher at the grocery store and suddenly realizing he had a life outside of school. Matt was a guy who studied science, made jokes, and planned Physics Club projects. Brinkley supposed it made sense that Matt would have a life beyond all that, that he might actually have a love life. She just hadn't stopped to think about it before.

Matt laughed. "Don't beat around the bush there, Emma! Get right to the point!"

"I'm sorry," Brinkley said, blushing slightly again. "I was just curious."

"No big deal. Besides, if it makes you feel any better, I'm pretty sure she doesn't know I'm alive."

"I wasn't trying to come on to you, Matt," she said. "I just don't know what I was thinking, dressing like this for this kind of party. I feel so conspicuous."

"It is a little on the tight side," he said. "Do you want to borrow this?" He pulled off his hoodie sweatshirt and handed it to her. Brinkley couldn't help but notice when he was taking it off that his T-shirt underneath got caught up in the hoodie, revealing for a second his abs and hip bones. Wow. Matt was kind of built.

"I couldn't," Brinkley said. Then she looked down at the baby tee and tight skirt hugging Emma's hips. "OK, maybe I could."

She pulled the hoodie over her other clothes. It smelled faintly of sandalwood and maybe a touch of vanilla. She hugged her arms around herself and said, "Thanks, Matt. You're the best."

Now that Brinkley felt a little less awkward, she looked around the room to see what everyone was doing. The dining hall wasn't much, just a large room with a linoleum floor and several tables. Brinkley helped put out the paper tablecloths and hang the banner. Then she and Matt blew up the balloons with the helium tank. Every so often, Matt would take a hit off the tank and do a hysterical rendition of the Lollypop Guild and Lullaby League songs from *The Wizard of Oz,* a movie that Brinkley could appreciate for its cinematic grandeur but had never personally liked because the flying monkeys had always given her nightmares. She'd never been around Matt much outside of class, but she had to admit he was kind of adorable.

"Guys, it's almost time for Dave to get here," said Jenna.

"Ooh! Are we supposed to hide and then jump out and yell 'Surprise!'?" asked Brinkley.

"Not unless you want to give him a heart attack," Jenna said. "We are talking about a World War II vet, Emma!" Brinkley found it interesting how Jenna's voice was full of good humor and not in the slightest bit sarcastic. If Brinkley had said something remotely similar to someone in her group of friends, there would've been an eye roll and a completely different tone of voice.

It was interesting how this group of people, who barely registered at all with anyone important, interacted with one another. Brinkley felt a little like one of those anthropologists who studied ancient tribes, living among them and learning their peculiar customs.

A minute later, one of the students came in, pushing an old man in a wheelchair. "Happy birthday, Dave!" everyone said, gathering around him and giving him hugs and handshakes. The smile on his face was unmistakable, although he seemed not quite sure who any of these people were.

"Emma," Jenna said, "why don't you sit next to Dave? After all, this party was your idea."

"It was?" Brinkley said.

"Well, yeah! Don't be so modest!"

"Oh, OK," Brinkley said. She moved over to a seat next to the man's wheelchair. Other residents began filing into the room, some in wheelchairs, others with walkers, a few on their own two feet. The young people greeted each of them warmly and began handing out cups of punch. Jenna led everyone in the birthday song, and Dave blew out the candles. There were only five or so on the cake. Brinkley figured that either no one knew his actual age or they didn't want to make him blow out nearly ninety candles. Dave had the first piece, and while he ate, he talked to Brinkley.

"I like you," he said. "You're a good girl. You remind me of my sweetheart back home."

"I do?" Brinkley said.

"Yes. We're going to get married and have some children when I get back."

"Oh," she said. "Well, that's great."

"It's nice of the USO to put on these parties for us," he said. "Takes your mind off things. Lying in these foxholes, next to the dead boys, and can't move for days, in the cold, the rain . . ." His eyes had a faraway look.

Brinkley took Dave's hand. "I'm sorry," she said. She meant it.

"Oh, these parties are awful nice," he said. "Makes me feel like myself again to come here and talk to a nice girl like you. It's hard being away from everybody and everything. A fella can just about forget who he is. Know what I mean?"

Brinkley smiled at Dave and gently squeezed his hand. "I think I do," she said.

chapter thirty-one

As anticipated, Brinkley woke up in her own bed the next morning. Jenna had driven her—Emma—home that night, all the way out to a farmhouse in the middle of nowhere, and Brinkley, knowing the drill, had gone right in, lain on Emma's bed, and fallen asleep. It hadn't been the kind of party she'd anticipated, not by any means, but it had been fun in its own way. Doing something nice for that old man had given her an unusual feeling, a good one. Different than, say, being featured on the Snapshot page of *Teen Vogue* (which, make no mistake, had been delicious), but still very nice.

And not only that, it had been peculiarly pleasant to receive the kind of attention Emma received. Brinkley was used to people fawning all over her about how beautiful she was. The cadre of simpering admirers who showed due reverence for her fashion sense and perfect features was something she'd always enjoyed. But this shtick Emma was working . . . now that was something. People seemed to look up to her merely because she was a nice person. Brinkley found it quaint. Being Emma had been like a short vacation where one stays in a charming cottage instead of a five-star hotel. Different, but good.

When she heard the hum of the garage door opening, she rolled over and looked at the clock. It was six in the morning. It had to be Miranda, returning her car.

Brinkley threw on her robe and went running down the stairs to the garage. Miranda had left the keys on the hood and had started walking down the driveway.

"Miranda! Wait!" Brinkley yelled.

Miranda turned around and said, "What? Are you going to call the cops on me?"

Brinkley wasn't even interested in gaining the upper hand. "You were totally right. I was totally wrong. Just accept my apology, please."

Miranda looked quizzical. "For real?"

"For real. I'm sorry."

"Wow. This out-of-body stuff really is doing a number on you," she said. "Copacetic. You're forgiven. Now spill it. What happened?"

"Emma Paulis is nice. She's really, extremely, disgustingly non-fake nice. I'm kind of sick just thinking about how anyone could be that nice," Brinkley said. "And I completely violated her by not respecting the fact that I was walking around in her body, and I made her look bad, and that was wrong. There. Happy?"

"Am I supposed to absolve you now, or what?"

"I don't know. Maybe."

"Consider yourself absolved, then."

"Are you going to stay mad at me?" Brinkley asked. "Or are we friends again?"

"We were friends?"

The question gave Brinkley pause. "Well . . . yeah. Weren't we?"

"If you say so. As long as we don't have to do one of those girly hugs and squeal now."

"No reason to get carried away," Brinkley said, nudging Miranda with her shoulder. "I mean, you're still a freakbag."

"That's good to hear. I didn't want to accidentally turn into a prep by association."

"But I'll give you a ride to school, if you're not afraid that being seen with me will kill your rep with the other freaks."

"I guess I'll take the risk," said Miranda.

"And I'm driving you to work today, right?"

"If you can still fit it in with all your activities. You know, like the school play, and, of course, that ritualistic flashing of female thighs to the gods of the little brown ball. I believe the proper term for that is 'cheerleading'?"

"Oh, just stop," Brinkley said. "Ritualistic thigh flashing practice is on a different day. Help yourself to anything in the kitchen while I get ready."

When they arrived at Story High, people stood speechless as Brinkley and Miranda walked from the parking lot to the building together.

"So much for your rep," Brinkley whispered.

"So much for yours," Miranda replied.

Just then, Bette yanked Brinkley by the arm and spat out in a loud whisper, "What are you *doing?*"

Brinkley jerked her arm away. "I'm going to my locker. And why are you trying to rip my arm off?"

Bette pulled her aside so no one would hear. "Look, there's being cordial to psychos so they won't stab you, and then there's crossing the line into palling around with them. You can't let people see you with her! They'll think you're friends or something."

"Take a pill, Bette," said Brinkley. "We are friends."

"You're not serious," Bette said. "You can't be friends with *her!*"

"Oh, relax already. You're still my BFF."

"I don't know what's been going on with you lately, Brinks. You've practically dropped off the face of the planet in the past couple of weeks, and nobody ever knows where you are, and now you're hanging around with losers."

"She's not a loser. If you'd just take the time to get to know her—"

"I'd rather spend my time getting the old Brinkley back!" said Bette. "And I know just how to do it! Tristan's party tonight!"

"Tristan's party? Tonight?"

"Yeah. What? You act like you hadn't heard about it. Surely Tristan told you, right?"

"Of course," Brinkley lied.

"So, I'll come by your house and we'll get ready. Some guys from the university are supposed to be there. Fraternity guys! I've got to look hot!"

"I'm sure it will be fun," Brinkley said, mostly to convince herself.

Brinkley found Tristan at his locker before the bell rang. "Why didn't you tell me you were having a party tonight?"

"Chill, babe," Tristan said. "It was kind of last minute. Just planned it yesterday. I was going to tell you, but you never answered your phone or replied to my texts."

He has a point, Brinkley thought. "I've been busy," she said.

"It's cool. It's at the lake house. I found out from my parents that the neighbors are going to be in Europe, so nobody's going to call the cops on us if we get loud. It'll be the party of the year! And some guys from the top frats are coming, so I can network for rush next year. Not that I need it, but it never hurts to come out of the gate strong."

"Sure," Brinkley said to Tristan, only half listening.

"Oh, and, babe," Tristan said, pressing her up against the lockers, "wear something sexy for me, OK?" He kissed her neck. "I've been missing you. We need to get reacquainted."

Matt Baker walked by just then and looked away quickly, as though he didn't want to see them. Brinkley felt embarrassed, but didn't know exactly why. "I've got to get to class," she told Tristan, pushing him away.

"Tonight, babe!" Tristan called after her. "You and me!"

chapter thirty-two

*B*rinkley's after-school schedule was packed that Friday: First, she had to drop Miranda off at work. Then, she had to go back to school for rehearsal. After that, an appointment with Irirangi at six o'clock (on a Friday evening! The woman was relentless!). Then she had some shopping to do, then the party, and last, she'd have to pick up Miranda from work around eleven, which meant she'd have to leave the party a bit early, but she didn't mind that. She could manage it all, no problem . . . provided no pesky jumps interfered with her plans.

She'd invited Bette to go shopping, but Bette had announced she'd made plans with her mom. Bette was generally outspoken about her dislike for her mother, but Brinkley figured that maybe Bette was following her advice and trying to be nicer to people. They'd arranged to meet at Brinkley's around eight and ride to the party together from there.

Traffic was a little worse than Brinkley had anticipated, so she was a few minutes late to rehearsal after dropping Miranda off at Ireland's Kitchen. Emma was already onstage. They were working on scene five, in which Laura made a wish on the moon. A few days ago, Brinkley would've immediately made her presence known and demanded that Emma relinquish the stage to the real star. But now, Brinkley stood quietly in the back, watching. Laura had few lines in this scene. It was mostly an exchange between Laura's mother and brother. But, even though Laura didn't have much to say, it struck Brinkley that Emma brought the character to life simply in the way she held her posture and walked into the room holding a dish towel. Without saying more than a few words, Emma channeled Laura in a way that Brinkley hadn't imagined before. All at once, the point of the play made sense to Brinkley. Laura Wingfield was a delicate girl who could never truly live in the real world. That's what all that stuff about the glass unicorn had been about. Brinkley had been playing the part all wrong. Mr. Ellis should have been more insistent in his direction. How could he have let her ruin the play like that?

Everything Miranda had said the day she dropped off her costume rushed back to her. Brinkley had gotten the part only because of her family's money. She'd been allowed to butcher the role because she was a mean, nasty girl who decimated anyone who dared cross her.

This was Emma's part. It had been Emma's part all along.

Mr. Ellis interrupted her thoughts just as scene five ended. "Brinkley! You're here. Great," he said. *You'd think with all that acting background, Ellis might be a little more convincing,* Brinkley thought. "Come on up. Emma was just filling in."

Brinkley forced her legs to walk her to the stage. "Mr. Ellis, I was thinking . . ." she began.

"So was I, Brinkley!" he said. "I was thinking how wonderful it's going to be to have your parents here to see the first production in our new theater, with your grandmother's name on it, and with you in the lead role. Will your entire family be coming?"

"I . . . I don't know."

"Oh, I do hope so. I want to thank them personally for their generosity. Let's take five and then pick up with scene seven, where Jim remembers calling Laura 'Blue Roses.'"

As the cast members and crew shuttled about the stage, Brinkley made her way to Emma, who was removing an apron and putting it back with the costumes. "Emma, about your performance just now," Brinkley said.

"Oh, I'm sorry, Brinkley. I hope you don't mind. Mr. Ellis insisted I fill in, as your understudy, until you got back."

"No, I don't mind. In fact, I just wanted to say that you were wonderful."

Emma looked astonished. "Thank you, Brinkley," she said. "That's very nice of you to say." The words almost begged to be followed up with, *What in the world has gotten into you?*

"I mean it. You're a terrific actress. Much better than I am. You should've gotten this part."

"Don't be silly," Emma said. "I'm sure you'll be great."

"Emma, I want you to have the part. Really. You deserve it."

"Brinkley," Emma said, "that's extremely generous of you, but I couldn't possibly. I wouldn't feel right about it. Mr. Ellis chose you because he thought you were the best person for the role, and I couldn't let you give up such a fantastic opportunity. You'll be great. I just know it."

Perhaps Emma was right. When rehearsal continued, Brinkley's performance was much improved. She understood Laura better and gave her characterization more of the nuances the part called for.

"Brinkley, that was incredible," Mr. Ellis said at the end of practice. "Your performance today was—dare I say it?—inspired. I can see that you've really been working on the role."

"I guess," she replied.

"You seem to be getting at the heart of what it means to be an actor, to leave oneself behind and emerge as a completely new individual. And you've progressed so quickly!"

But Brinkley knew who the role really belonged to.

⸎

"What's the matter, Brinkley?" Irirangi asked when Brinkley sat down for their appointment. "Are you mad because I made you come for a session on a Friday evening?"

"It's not that," Brinkley said.

"Then what?"

"You know that part I got in the school play? Well, turns out, I didn't deserve it. I've been playing the part wrong the whole time. Totally wrong. They only gave me the part because my family paid for the new theater."

"And it upset you to learn this today?"

"Well, of course. Wouldn't it upset you?"

"Yes. Yes, it would. But when we first met, you didn't seem to have a problem with your family's money and influence making your path smoother in life. Nor did you feel that your physical beauty was an undeserved advantage," Irirangi said. "And surely, you weren't under the impression prior to today that you had been awarded the part based on your dedication to acting?"

"I thought he'd picked me to star in the play because I was the prettiest," Brinkley said. "That's so stupid. The role doesn't even call for a particularly pretty girl. I just thought . . . oh, I don't know what I thought. I guess I just hadn't considered what it might mean to Emma, my understudy, to get that part. You should've seen her today. She deserves to play Laura Wingfield, not me."

"May I tell you what I just heard you say?"

"Huh?"

"You just said, 'I hadn't considered what it might mean to Emma.' Brinkley, do you realize what happened to you today?"

"I felt like a complete idiot?"

"No. Well, yes . . . but no. What you experienced today, Brinkley, was empathy. You thought about Emma's feelings. You put yourself in her place. Do you realize how remarkable that is?"

"If you say so."

"This is a real breakthrough. I'm extremely proud of your progress. I can't even tell you how thrilled I am."

"Whoopee," Brinkley said, circling an index finger in the air. "Glad my humiliation brings you such joy."

"I take no delight in your pain, Brinkley. But emotional pain is highly underrated. When we feel negative emotions, such as guilt or sadness, they can be a powerful catalyst for positive behavior. Have you ever considered that your disdain for others might be a defense mechanism to help you deal with your trust issues?"

"I have trust issues?"

"What do you think?"

"Oh, here we go again," Brinkley said. "Why do I have to answer all the questions? You're the one with the formal training. Why don't you just tell me what's wrong with me?" She stopped a minute. "You do have formal training, don't you?"

Irirangi smiled. "The very best. Though some may find my methods a bit unorthodox. But we're not here to talk about me."

"All right. I guess we can get back to grilling me some more."

"Back to the issue of trust, then. Why don't you list for me the people you trust?"

Brinkley didn't say anything.

"Your parents?"

"I don't want to talk about my parents," Brinkley said.

"Then that's probably a good reason to talk about them, don't you think?"

"Look, my parents are just kind of into their own thing. They work a lot. I don't know why they even decided to have a kid. Maybe it was an accident. Or a mistake. Notice they didn't have any more after me. But it's not like they put me up for adoption."

"Not being put up for adoption isn't much of a basis for filial affection."

"They provide for me. I have the best of everything. They're paying for these sessions with you. They're always harping on how I have to get into a good college. They don't hit me or anything. They love me in their own way."

"Do they pay attention to you?" Irirangi asked.

Brinkley looked away from Irirangi and fixated her gaze on a vase. "In eighth grade, there was this girl, Janie. She was new. I liked her a lot. We got to be really good friends. One time, I went to her house for a sleepover, and we sneaked out and TP'ed one of the teachers' yards. It was my idea. We didn't do it to be mean, just for laughs. We were fourteen, I guess. Anyway, her mom caught us sneaking back in, and her parents went ballistic. They sat us both down and preached for like, an hour, about how dangerous it was for girls to sneak out at night, how anything could've happened to us, and then they grounded her for a month."

"And what did your parents do?"

"I don't think they ever even found out. Tallulah picked me up the next morning, and Janie's parents told her, but if she ever told my folks, I never heard anything about it."

"And your friendship with Janie?"

"You know those four girls who left school because of me? Janie makes five. Her parents never complained to the school about me or anything, but she left after we stopped being friends. I made sure of it."

"I see."

"She took it for months before they moved her to another school."

"Were you angry that her parents punished her, and yours did nothing?"

"Why would I be angry about that? That's nuts."

"An adolescent's job is to push the parents' boundaries. A parent's job is to enforce them. It's a balanced give-and-take relationship. When the parent doesn't push back, the adolescent feels insecure. Subconsciously, children deeply need and desire parental authority in order to feel safe in the world."

"So you're saying that I wanted my parents to ground me? Lady, that stuff they're teaching you in shrink school is wack!"

"Brinkley, who is your best friend?" Irirangi asked.

"Bette."

"And do you trust Bette?"

"Sure."

"Do you tell her everything?"

"Of course. Mostly."

Irirangi just sat there, looking at her. Brinkley continued, "Nobody tells anybody *everything,* right? I mean, that's just stupid. But Bette's great. We've been friends since middle school. She's the best. I trust her completely."

Maybe not completely, Brinkley thought. *But close enough.* Bette had never given her any reason to doubt her loyalty.

"One of the scariest things about life, Brinkley, is this: the only way to ever really know if you can trust someone is to give that person the opportunity to violate your trust."

"Why would you ever want to put yourself in that position?" Brinkley asked.

"Because that vulnerability is an essential component of the most valuable thing in life, the one thing every person on the planet seeks: love."

"So you're saying you have to give people the chance to screw you over if you want love?"

"Love can't exist without trust. And trust can't exist without vulnerability. The very reason love is so precious is because it's something we can lose, at deep personal cost. That's why it's so valuable. It's what everyone wants." Irirangi's voice softened. "Even you."

Brinkley felt uncomfortable. "Look, our hour is up. I have some shopping to do."

"Shopping." Irirangi sighed. "That sounds like the old Brinkley."

"Have you seen the new Tory Burch totes? They're to die for!"

"You may go, Brinkley."

The handbag Brinkley selected at the boutique was a steal at just under five hundred dollars, and just what the doctor ordered for someone who deserved it so much.

When she got home, she called Tallulah, who came in from the laundry room. "Is there anything you need?" Tallulah asked.

"No, not a thing," Brinkley said. "But there's something you need." She handed her a wrapped package.

"For me?" Tallulah asked.

"Of course for you!" Brinkley said. "Open it!"

Tallulah took the bright yellow purse from the tissue paper. "It's so pretty!" she said. "But . . ."

"And look! It has little gold T's at the base of the straps. T for Tallulah!"

"But . . . why?"

"Because you're wonderful to me," Brinkley said. "You always have been. And I'm sorry I never appreciated it before. But I will from now on."

Brinkley thought she saw Tallulah's eyes well up, but Tallulah looked away too soon for her to be sure. "I'll like carrying it," Tallulah said, "because it came from you. Thank you."

"Come look in the mirror!" said Brinkley. She pulled Tallulah to the hallway mirror, put the bag's straps on her shoulder, and turned her sideways. "It's totally you! But you'll need just the right outfit and shoes to go with it. And maybe a new hairdo. Pick a day next week and we'll go shopping, and to the salon."

"You and I?"

"It'll be fun!" Brinkley checked her watch. "I've got to get ready for a party." Somewhat awkwardly, she kissed Tallulah on the cheek before heading upstairs.

She'd thought about not going. Seriously. But it was sure to be the party of the year, or at least the week, and she didn't want to hear about it from everyone else at school on Monday. She needed to make an appearance. She'd have to avoid Tristan for sure, but that shouldn't be too hard given that the place would be packed. Bette would be there, and a lot of cute college guys, so it might be fun. Besides, she'd have to ditch out to pick up Miranda anyway.

What to wear? The fact that Tristan had requested something sexy made her want to reach for a pilgrim's dress or a nun's habit, but neither of those options hung in her closet. For some reason, anything she put on made her breasts seem more prominent than usual—weird. She ended up going with a simple belted shirt and black leggings. Coverage plus cool. Her phone buzzed. She picked it up to see a text from Bette:

WHAT R U WEARING 2NITE?

Like she was going to tell Bette. Bette would either copy her or outdress her.

NOT SURE. U?

Bette replied:

TRYING 2 DCIDE B/T RED & BLK MINIDRESS OR
BLU SILK JMPR.

Though she actually did laugh out loud at the thought of anyone wearing silk to such an occasion, Brinkley was never one to type LOL, which she regarded as banal.

MINIDRESS. U WILL RUIN SILK WHEN U THROW UP ON IT.

Bette, not above banality, replied:

LOL! UR RT! SHOWING PLENTY OF LEG EITHER WAY SO WILL GO W/
DRESS!!! C U SOON!

But Brinkley did not see Bette soon. By eight thirty, she hadn't shown up and wasn't answering her phone or returning Brinkley's texts. Brinkley texted Tristan:

IS BETTE THERE?

He responded:

THOUGHT SHE WAS W/ U.

Some help he was. Brinkley called Bette's mom. "She's gone to bed, Brinkley," Mrs. Caravallo said. "I'm afraid she's not feeling well."

"I hope her getting sick didn't interfere with your shopping trip," Brinkley said.

"Shopping trip? I just got home from work a little while ago."

"Oh. I thought Bette had told me you two were going shopping. I guess I misunderstood."

Interesting. Bette would have to be on her deathbed to miss a party like this. What was she up to? There was only one way for Brinkley to find out.

chapter thirty-three

*W*hen she arrived at Tristan's lake house, there were already about twenty teenagers standing around outside. One was funneling beer while about half a dozen egged him on, one girl was vomiting under a tree while a boy held her hair back, and the rest were just standing around talking much more loudly than necessary, as drunk people tended to do.

Brinkley had to park far down the road because there were so many cars. As she walked up the path, groups of guys she didn't recognize, some in shirts with Greek letters, looked at her like dogs sizing up a morsel. Some of the drunker ones whistled. One or two offered a "hey baby" mating call, which Brinkley, of course, ignored.

"Babe!" Tristan called. He pushed past the crowd near the keg. "You made it! Mmmm . . . you do look hot."

His breath smelled sour and dank, like whiskey and clogged sinuses. He slipped his hand under her shirt and caressed the small of her back. "Let's go upstairs, where it's more private."

Brinkley moved his hand. "I just got here."

"Right. Here, have this." Before she knew it, he'd lifted a bottle to her mouth and was pouring a menthol-flavored liquid down her throat.

Brinkley pushed it away. "I'm driving, you idiot!"

Tristan just laughed.

"You've poured it all over me! Look at my shirt!"

"You're right," he said. "I think you should definitely take it off! Especially because, if I may say so . . ." Tristan burped, then finished his thought. "Your boobs look huge tonight!" Then he yelled, "Who wants to see my girlfriend take off her shirt?" The partygoers cheered and hooted.

"Dream on!" Brinkley said. She stomped to the bathroom down the hall, but found it occupied. She waited and waited, calling and banging on the door, but no one came out, and the door was locked. Probably someone had passed out in there or a random just-for-tonight couple was making out. Brinkley sighed. She thought about Dave's birthday party, and how she'd felt so comfortable once she'd borrowed Matt's hoodie, just talking and hanging out with people. No one there had to be drunk to feel relaxed. Here, everyone was trying to act like adults, but they were like adults on some reality-television show—obnoxious and self-conscious. The kind of pathetic adults people her age would laugh about right up until they became them.

Brinkley made her way upstairs to Tristan's guest room, which, surprisingly, was unoccupied. She grabbed a shirt out of his drawer and, after making sure the door was locked, changed out of her soaked top.

What was that stuff he'd made her drink? She hadn't swallowed much of it, but she was beginning to feel lightheaded. He hadn't roofied her, had he? *No way,* she thought. *Tristan is slimy, but not that slimy.* She needed to lie down. She opened the door and saw Pablo, a guy from the football team—a good, trustworthy guy—going down the stairs. "Pablo," she called.

"Yeah, Brinkley? Hey, you don't look so good."

"I'm not feeling all that well. Look, I need to lie down. Will you make sure nobody, you know, bothers me?"

"Sure, sure, Brinkley. You want me to get you a glass of water or something?"

"No, I just need to rest a minute. I'm not sure what I drank. I just don't feel right."

"No worries. I'll keep an eye on you," Pablo said. "I'll even drive you home if you want."

Drive you home. That reminded her: Miranda. She had to pick up Miranda from work. But there was plenty of time before that. She'd just rest for a little until she felt better. She lay down on the bed and closed her eyes.

chapter thirty-four

There you are, you naughty girl!" the guy was whispering, and, still half asleep, Brinkley couldn't tell who it was. Her body felt slightly contorted: she was partially sitting up, and something felt cold against the small of her back. But the cold was quickly replaced by the warmth of his hand against her skin as he began caressing her. "I wondered where you'd disappeared to." She couldn't see anything in the dark.

"Get off me!" she demanded. Now she remembered where she was supposed to be. But there was no soft bed underneath her—and where was Pablo? Hadn't she asked him to look out for her? Even without being able to see, Brinkley felt a strange familiarity about this invasion. That cologne . . . notes of oak moss and leather, a bit powdery-Dior Homme. "Tristan! What do you think you're doing?" Tristan continued kissing her neck and running his hands over her back. "Giving you what you want," he whispered.

Brinkley pushed him away and struggled to get up, frantically running her hands along the walls for a light switch. She felt cold porcelain and marble. Her hands traced a faucet and sink. A bathroom. Where were they? And what time was it? She had to pick up Miranda from work just after eleven. Tristan slithered up to her again in the darkness. "Look, would you get off of me already? I've got to go."

"I love it when you play hard to get," Tristan said, pulling her into an embrace.

"Tristan, so help me, I'll have you singing soprano for the rest of your life if you don't take your hands off me right now!"

Tristan's whispery voice became a shrill whine. "What's your problem? You think I don't get enough of this already? Honey, if I needed the ice-princess routine, I'd know where to go."

Not that ice-princess crap again. It was as though he'd learned one metaphor in his life and was going to milk it for every last drop.

"Poor baby. Save it. I told you, I don't have time."

"You're so bitchy," Tristan said. "You're starting to sound just like Brinkley."

She processed his words.

If Tristan hadn't meant to get his freak on with *her* in a darkened bathroom, then just who *was* he picking up a little action from? And how long had these little Tristan trysts been going on behind her back, anyway? Who did this guy think he was, cheating on her? And what girl at Story High would be foolish enough to risk the wrath of Brinkley Harper? Finally, she found the light switch and flicked it on. She looked down. Shiny brown locks fell to her shoulders, and a red-and-black minidress hugged her every curve.

There in the mirror above the sink, her best friend's reflection looked back at her. "It's OK, baby," Tristan said. "I forgive you. Now turn out those lights and let's get back to business."

She knocked Tristan aside and threw open the door to storm downstairs. Tristan followed close behind.

"Did I do something?" he asked, racing to keep up with her.

"How could you?" she said. Then, remembering she was Bette, said, "How could you do that to my best friend?"

"Excuse me, but I seem to recall that you were the one who started this over a month ago," he replied. "And don't give me that 'best-friend' crap. You're always complaining about how you can't stand Brinkley and how she's *soooo* self-absorbed and she's not half as pretty as she thinks she is. Don't talk to me about your best frenemy."

Brinkley's mind raced. "What else have I said about Brinkley?"

"What do you mean?"

"I mean . . . you know. . . ." Brinkley searched for the best way to pry information out of Tristan without sounding crazy. She moved in closer to him and ran her index finger along his torso. "What's your favorite dirty little secret about Brinkley?"

Tristan softened instantly. "Well, I thought it was pretty funny about how she wet the bed until she was ten."

She told him that? How could she!? Brinkley faked a laugh. "You know I just made that up, though, right? It's not true. Not at all!"

"Whatever, baby," Tristan said. "Why are we wasting time talking about Brinkley? Let's go back upstairs. You know you're crazy about me."

None of this made any sense. She pushed Tristan away again. "If you like me, why don't you just break up with Brinkley?"

Tristan grinned. "You know we both like the danger."

"And you like having two girls instead of one," she said, wanting to add, *And while you're stupid, you're not stupid enough to dump the hottest girl in school.*

"You know Brinkley means nothing to me. We're a tabloid couple," he said. "It's strictly for publicity."

"That's true," she said. "Plus, she doesn't even find you attractive."

"What?" Tristan said. "What do you mean? Of course she finds me attractive."

Brinkley enjoyed getting in the dig, but Miranda would be wait-ing. "I've gotta go."

Brinkley was getting into her car when Pablo stopped her. "Bette!" he called, jogging over. "That's Brinkley's car, isn't it?"

"Um, yeah. Yeah, it is. I'm borrowing it. BFFs share and share alike, you know."

"Does she know you're sharing her boyfriend, too?" Pablo asked. "That's not cool, Bette."

At least someone around here had some sense of decency. "You're right. It's not. I was just going to find her and apologize."

"I've been looking for her for the past half hour. She wasn't feeling so good earlier, and I was trying to look out for her, but it's like she just disappeared. You're not taking her car and leaving her here, are you?"

"Of course not. Would I do something like that?" *Yes,* Brinkley thought. *The correct answer is, yes, Bette would totally do something like that.*

The look on Pablo's face showed that he knew the correct answer too. "So where do you think she is, then?"

"Oh, she left," Brinkley said. "She didn't feel up to driving, so she caught a ride home with . . . with . . . Emma Paulis." She was the first person who popped into Brinkley's head.

"Emma Paulis was at this party?" Pablo looked doubtful.

"Well, she wasn't exactly at the party. . . . She . . . offered a sort of taxi service to anyone who needed it as part of her service club's efforts to curb drunk driving."

"Now that sounds like Emma," Pablo said. "OK, then. As long as she's all right. Tell Brinkley that next time, she could let me know she's leaving so I don't freak out looking for her. I take babysitting duties seriously."

"You're a good guy, Pablo," Brinkley said.

"That's what my mom keeps telling me. Drive safe, now."

❦

Miranda was sitting outside the restaurant when Brinkley pulled up. When Miranda saw Bette in the car, she said, "What are you doing here?"

Brinkley couldn't resist having a little fun with her. "I thought we could hang out!"

"Where's Brinkley? Why do you have her car?"

"Brinkley couldn't make it. I thought we could have a sleepover at my house, paint our toenails, and tell each other our deepest, darkest secrets!"

Miranda studied her for a moment. Then, a huge grin spread across her face. "You're kidding!"

Brinkley shook her head.

"Priceless," Miranda said. "I'm almost jealous. I could do some serious damage in that situation. Oh, wait, I forgot. She's, *like, totally your BFF!*" She sneered. "Paranormal experiences are always wasted on the wrong people."

"Not always," Brinkley replied. "Turns out I'm learning a lot about who my friends are. She's been seeing my boyfriend behind my back, and if she'd sink that low, who knows what else?"

"You do realize we're talking about the same person who wrote a series of passionate love letters to Coach Freedman our freshman year and signed them from me, don't you?"

"Oh, man—I'd forgotten about that!" Brinkley almost laughed but caught herself. "That was pretty evil, huh?"

"I had to get special permission to sign up for marching band in the middle of the year and have it count as my health and fitness credit. I don't even play an instrument, so I had to carry a flag on the field and just stand there while everyone else played music. Do you have any idea how humiliating that was? But it was still better than having to listen to everyone hum "I Kissed a Girl" to me while Coach Freedman took roll in PE."

Brinkley remembered. It had all seemed so hilarious in ninth grade. "I had no idea. I'm so sorry. I should've stopped her."

"She's a turbo bitch," Miranda said, "but luckily, fate—or a supernatural force—has dealt you this opportunity to even the score. Question is, how do we make the most of it?"

"I don't know, but I'm not falling asleep until we figure it out," Brinkley said. "Are you up for Starbucks?"

"Nobody's waiting up for me at home," Miranda said. "This is shaping up to be the best Friday night I've ever had!"

⚜

Brinkley and Miranda ordered two double espressos and started a list on a napkin. The first item was, *Shave her head,* Miranda's suggestion. "Seriously! Just go full-on crazy Britney!"

Second was, *Have breast implants removed,* which Brinkley vetoed. "We'd have to book that weeks in advance. I can't stay awake that long."

Other items included giving away all Bette's designer clothes to charity, making out with the first (and only) chair of the French horn section of the school band, and getting a large neck tattoo of Hannah Montana.

While they were conferring, a couple of girls approached their table. "Bette, what are you doing here?"

Brinkley looked up at Lauren and Kathryn, two girls from the cheerleading squad. "Getting coffee. What else?"

"OK, what I meant was, what are you *doing* here?" said Kathryn, nodding toward Miranda.

"Oh," Brinkley said. "Oh! Right! You're surprised to see me with Miranda!" She and Miranda smiled at each other. "I was just trying to see if she knew of any like, alternative methods for getting rid of cellulite. My butt is like cottage cheese!"

"Ewww!" Lauren and Kathryn said.

"Yep. That's right," Brinkley said. "There are more craters on my butt than on the surface of the moon. And I'm not ashamed of who knows it! In fact, you can tell everyone at school, and I won't even mind!"

"Seriously?" said Lauren.

"Yep. My mission is to raise awareness about cellulite," Brinkley said, while Miranda tried to contain her laughter. "The only way to fight this condition is to come forward and speak out!"

"Where's Brinkley?" asked Kathryn.

"Oh," Brinkley said. "Yeah. I think she's sick or something."

"She was at Tristan's party earlier," said Lauren. "Seems like she wasn't there very long, though."

"Maybe she had an emergency appointment for a chemical peel," said Kathryn. "I paid attention after you pointed it out, and you were right, Bette, her pores are *huge!*"

"Really! You could fall inside one and never be seen again!" said Lauren.

Just before Brinkley jumped out of her seat to bitch-slap the both of them, Miranda kicked her under the table. Brinkley put on a fake smile. "Did I really say such an awful thing?" She tinged her voice with sarcasm so they'd feel free to spill more info.

"Of course, not, dear, sweet Bette!" Kathryn said. "You'd never say such a thing! You'd never say that Brinkley's pores were big or that she sucked as cheerleading captain!" Brinkley squeezed her coffee cup so hard it folded, spilling coffee everywhere. Kathryn said, "Bette! Watch out!"

"Flimsy cups," Brinkley said.

"Anyway," said Lauren, "I heard that the reason Brinkley left the party so early was because Tristan tired her out, if you know what I mean."

"Where did you hear that?"

"From Tristan! He said she couldn't get enough."

"And you believed him?" said Brinkley.

"Well, yeah. I mean, after you told us that she's a nympho, of course we believe him!"

Brinkley gripped the table and urged herself to calm down. They'd be sorry. Oh, the fire she would rain down upon their heads! She folded the napkin list, and bided her time. "Well, we'd love to stay and chat," Brinkley said, "but Miranda and I have to go."

"Where are you going?" Kathryn asked.

"To shave my head," Brinkley replied.

"Shave your head? Bette, are you crazy?"

"It's got to be done. It keeps down the lice," Miranda said.

Nice one! thought Brinkley.

"Bette, you have lice?" Lauren said.

"Those little suckers just love me!" Brinkley said. "Almost as much as I love you guys!" She pulled them both in for a hug. Lauren and Kathryn pulled away as if from a hot stove. When Brinkley and Miranda turned to look at them as they walked out the door, both Lauren and Kathryn were shivering from a bad case of the willies.

"You're going to do the Britney!" Miranda said when they got in the car. "Awesome! Oh, please, please—let me do the honors!" Miranda mimicked shaving Bette's head and made a *nnnrrrrrrrrr* sound.

"Let's go to Bette's house first. Take a look around. With an opportunity like this, it's best not to be hasty."

Bette's was a climber's home: One of the smaller dwellings on the outskirts of a tony neighborhood, a place where the not-so-rich-but-hopeful bought to give the impression they were in the same league as families like the Harpers. It was the kind of house a sensible family like the Ingrams would pass up in favor of one with more room for the same money in a less stylish part of town. Bette's dad sold insurance and did fairly well, and her mom was in real estate. The furnishings were passable but not high quality, and Bette's mother kept the place up to date with trendy paint. Both of Bette's parents were asleep and didn't notice that Bette had come in just before midnight with a new friend.

"You can tell a lot about a person from her room," Miranda said.

Brinkley thought of Miranda's room, barren except for the little sanctuary. "Like what?"

"For instance, this room has a built-in bookcase with very few books. No pleasure reading, only paperbacks required for school. But the vanity, here, is cluttered with expensive products." She picked up a bottle. "What's this? Probably thirty bucks from Sephora?"

"Eighty, actually."

"Hope in a bottle, as they say. And take a look at this." Miranda pointed to the magazine clippings that were tacked up on the walls around the vanity—detailed hairstyles and makeup tips, and several "Five Pieces, Fifteen Different Looks" spreads. "An altar to insecurity. She's consumed with worry at all times about how she looks, about trying to look like she has more money than she does."

"Man, you're good," Brinkley said. "I don't know why I never saw it before. What are you doing?"

Miranda was opening drawers and rifling through the contents. "Looking for a diary. I happen to be a graduate of eBay University!" she sang. "Wonder how much people at Story would pay for a peek?" She found a lavender-colored book in between the mattress and box springs. "Pay dirt!"

"I don't think we should be doing this," Brinkley said.

"You're just saying that to sound ethical. You know you want to."

"I know. Go ahead."

Miranda opened the book to a random page in the middle. "'Brinkley's gymnastics skills are nowhere near as good as mine. I should be head of the squad. She totally sucks at it. Plus, she's not really that pretty, if you look at her long enough. Tristan agrees. Today, he told me I was way hotter than Brinkley. He called me last night at eleven-thirty and got me to sneak out with him. He took me to his lake house, and he'd fixed a picnic, with candles and everything, just for us. I know he loves me. I can feel it in my heart!'"

"When did she write that?" Brinkley asked.

"About three weeks ago."

"Figures. He called me one night about three weeks ago and told me he wanted me to sneak out and go to his lake house with him. He said he'd set up a candlelight picnic for me. I said no."

"I wonder how many other girls he called before he got to Bette." Miranda leafed through the pages. "Pretty much everything in here looks like her insulting some other girl. Self-esteem issues, much? Man, this will go for a small fortune on eBay!"

"No, that's no good," Brinkley said.

"Yeah, that can wait. Let's get to the head shaving!"

"That's no good either," Brinkley said.

"What do you mean, it's no good? It's perfect! It's the ideal counterstrike—hit her where it hurts! I just said she's obsessed with her looks, and nobody looks good bald!" Miranda paused. "Well, maybe the lead singer of Disturbed . . . and babies . . . but certainly not Bette."

"I already know the ideal punishment for Bette," Brinkley said.

"If it's better than head shaving, I want to hear it."

"Don't you see how lonely and desperate she is? The worst thing that could happen to Bette is that she has to wake up as Bette and be Bette all day long, every single day, for the rest of her life."

"I don't get it. What are you going to do to her?"

"Nothing."

"Nothing?"

"Not a thing."

"Are you crazy? After what she's done to you, the things she's said—you have the golden ticket for revenge in the palm of your hand, and you're going to let it slip away?"

"That's exactly what I'm going to do," Brinkley said.

"Maybe that works for you, but what about me? I've got a bit of an ax to grind here myself. You may have ascended to some great mountain of enlightenment because of your metaphysical experiences, but I haven't."

Brinkley looked Miranda in the eye. "OK," she said. "What do you want to do? Think of one thing—anything—that we can do to Bette right now that will make up for the way she's treated you, or even the score, or make you feel better."

Miranda looked at the floor.

"We're done here," Brinkley said. "Let's go."

"I know in the grand scheme of things, it wouldn't accomplish much," Miranda said, "but a little head shaving might make me feel just the tiniest bit better."

"Come on!"

Brinkley dropped Miranda at her house and watched as she sneaked into her bedroom window. Then she went home. Tallulah was pouring a glass of milk in the kitchen when she walked in.

"I hope I didn't startle you," Brinkley said. "Brinks is upstairs. She wanted me to come over and spend the night."

"Very good," Tallulah said, scurrying out of the kitchen.

Brinkley went upstairs, exhausted. Something buzzed in her pocket. Bette's cell. She looked at the screen. Tristan.

"Hello?"

"Baby, you still mad at me? Just tell me what I did."

"No." Let him twist on the rope he'd used to hang himself.

"Come on—just tell me how I can make it up to you."

"Meet me at the old paper mill at four o'clock this morning."

"That old abandoned place on the other side of town? It's kind of dangerous out there, isn't it?"

"Fine. Forget it."

"No, no . . . I'll do it, I'll do it."

Brinkley thought a moment. "And bring lobster."

"Lobster? Where am I going to get lobster at four o'clock in the morning?"

"That's your problem, isn't it?"

"OK, I'll bring lobster. Anything else?"

Brinkley tried to think of something difficult. "Yes, actually. I'd also like a coffee waffle cone from Ice Cream Hut."

"That's at least half an hour from the old mill! They close at nine anyway, and even if they didn't, it would melt before I could get it over there to you! And do they even have coffee ice cream?"

"Again, not my problem."

Tristan lowered his voice. "I can't say no to you, baby. Especially not with that husky voice you've got going tonight. Where'd that come from?"

Brinkley hadn't noticed, but Bette's voice did seem deeper than usual. Slightly reminiscent of Brenda Vicaro in *The Mirror Has Two Faces*. Apt title given the circumstances, Brinkley thought. "Probably the testosterone pills I've been taking."

"The what?"

"See you at four o'clock, loverboy." Or not.

She turned out the light and lay down on top of the comforter. If she was going to wake up in her own bed as herself anyway, she might as well get a head start.

But when Brinkley woke up that Saturday morning, she wasn't in her own bed. She looked around the room at four computer monitors and hundreds of cables. This wasn't right. Every time she'd jumped before, she'd woken up as though from a bizarre dream, fully herself again. She lifted the covers and looked down at her body.

Calmly, she got up and dialed a number on the cell phone plugged in next to the computers.

"Miranda," she said, "we have a problem. I'm a dude."

chapter thirty-five

*L*uckily, she was a dude who wore pajama pants to bed. "What am I going to do?" she asked Miranda.

Miranda couldn't help but laugh. "You woke up, as a dude, first thing in the morning. Do you have to pee?"

"Miranda!" Brinkley yelled. She hadn't even thought about that. But now that Miranda had mentioned it . . . oh, great.

"OK, OK . . . so you're Joe Schlossman?"

"How'd you know?"

"Duh . . . caller ID."

"Oh, yeah. I forgot."

"Of all the dudes to wake up as, you get stuck with Joe Schlossman. I mean, at least you could've turned into a guy whose junk you might want to check out."

"I am not checking out anyone's junk!" Brinkley hissed. She was still thinking about having to pee. "You're not helping!"

"Well, what do you want me to do?"

"I don't know," Brinkley said. She heard the doorbell ring.

"Joe, company!" called Mrs. Schlossman.

"I've gotta go," Brinkley said. "I'll keep you posted."

Brinkley opened a dresser drawer to find a T-shirt. Nope— underwear drawer. Brinkley closed it quickly. She didn't want the image of Joe Schlossman's briefs seared into her brain for eternity.

She opened the second drawer and hit pay dirt. She threw on the tee and went downstairs.

Matt Baker was standing there with two of his friends.

That's right, Brinkley thought. *Joe and Matt have been friends since middle school.*

"Nice hair," Matt said. "Very REO Speedwagon circa 1980." Brinkley put her hand on her head and felt the hair sticking out in a layered, curly sort of mullet. Right. This was how guys interacted with one another, by exchanging lighthearted insults.

"Yeah, well . . . your face looks like a . . ." She looked around the room, grasping. "An alien's!"

"Wow, feel the burn," one of the other guys said.

"You're not at your best when you first wake up, are you, Joe?" Matt said. " All the better for me to kick your butt at Rock Gods."

Brinkley didn't know the first thing about Rock Gods and was sorely whipped at each turn. Besides, who could concentrate on a video game when you had to pee so badly? She thought she would pop, but there was no way she was going to the bathroom. If only she could fall asleep. But that was impossible. No one could fall asleep feeling this much pain. "What is up with you today?" Matt asked. "Rough night or something?"

"Speaking of rough nights, I heard half the school got torn up at Tristan Phillips's party last night," said one of the other guys.

"Is that so?" Matt said. "So, who dares challenge me next? Brendan? James?"

Brendan said, "Yeah, and from the looks of some of the pictures I saw posted this morning, there were some hot-looking women with compromised inhibitions! Man, I knew I should've become a jock!"

"Yeah, and your mom would be chasing you all the way down the field with your inhaler. Now, who's playing?" said Matt.

"Quit changing the subject, Matt," James said. "I want to hear the scoop."

"Matt's just afraid we'll talk about the girl of his dreams."

"Shut up, Brendan." Matt never looked up from the screen.

"Sorry, man. The truth hurts. I heard she was there," Brendan said. "And you know what that means."

Matt turned away from the screen and stared at him. "No, Brendan, I don't know what that means. And I don't think you do, either, so why don't you take my advice and shut the hell up?"

"Bro, face the facts. Brinkley Harper's giving it to Tristan Phillips!" Brendan said.

"How dare you!" Brinkley shouted. The guys looked at her.

"What're you, her mom?" said James.

"She's totally giving it to him!" Brendan insisted.

"And how would you know?" Matt said.

"Everybody at school knows. Tristan told everybody. Where have you been?"

"And you believe Tristan Phillips?" Brinkley said.

"Why not?" Brendan began singing, "She's a supa-freak! Supa-freak! She's supa-freak-ay!"

"Shut *up*, Brendan!" Matt said.

"Back off, Brendan," James said. "Matt's been in love with her since ninth grade."

"I'm just messing with you," Brendan said. "Come on."

"One more word about her and I'll . . ." Matt said. "Just don't even say her name again, got it?"

"Or you'll what?" Brendan said. "You're not serious, man. Bros before hos!"

Matt's face was red, and he was gripping the controller so hard, his knuckles were white.

Brinkley saw her chance. In the movies, a good punch in the face would knock someone unconscious. It was the quickest way back to her own body. "Brinkley Harper is trash!" she said.

"What?" Matt said. "What's the matter with you?"

She got right up in Matt's face and called herself every ugly name she'd ever heard, until finally, Matt lost it. But he didn't punch Joe in the face. He merely shoved him.

The last thing Brinkley remembered thinking was, *I can't be knocked unconscious by a stupid shove,* just before the back of Joe's head hit the brick fireplace.

"Dude! Dude! Are you all right?" she heard Matt ask.

Then everything faded to black as a warm stream trickled down her leg.

chapter thirty-six

*W*hen she came to in her own bedroom, she felt the back of her head. Of course there was no bump. It was on Joe's head, not hers. Poor Joe. He didn't seem like the kind of guy who would say such horrible things about a girl. She felt sorry that she'd gotten his head knocked in and that for the rest of his life his friends would say, "Dude, remember that time you pissed yourself?" She wondered if he was OK.

She looked up Matt's cell number on his Facebook page and called him. "Hello?"

"Hi, Matt. It's Brinkley."

"Oh, hey. Hey, Brinkley. What's up?"

"Nothing much. What are you doing?"

"Actually, funny thing. I'm sitting in the emergency room."

"Are you all right?"

"I'm fine. I had an accident this morning with my friend Joe. He hit his head. I feel terrible about it."

"Is he going to be all right?"

"Yeah, just a mild concussion. The doctors say stuff like this happens all the time with guys horsing around. His mom's not too thrilled with me right now, but Joe said she'll get over it. I feel really bad."

"Matt, it wasn't your fault that he hit his head on the fireplace," she said.

"How'd you know he hit his head on the fireplace?"

"Oh . . . I . . . I saw it on somebody's wall on Facebook. That's why I looked up your number."

"Whose wall?"

"I forget. So many people commented on it that I lost track of the original thread. Well, listen, if you're not doing anything tonight, I wondered if you'd like to attend opening night of the school play with me."

"With you? I thought you were the star. You can't very well sit out in the audience with me, can you?" Matt asked. "And besides, don't you think your boyfriend might have a problem with that?"

"I don't have a boyfriend," Brinkley said.

"Really? As of when?"

"As of about five seconds after I get off the phone with you," she said. "If you don't mind complete honesty."

Matt laughed. "OK, Brinkley. I'll be your rebound escort, I guess. What time should I pick you up?"

"How about if I meet you there? I need to get there early."

"You're not going to stand me up again, are you?"

Brinkley hoped not. "Not if I can help it."

"I'll have to take my chances, I guess. See you there."

As promised, Brinkley called Tristan as soon as she hung up with Matt. She got his voice mail. He was probably somewhere with Bette making up for lost time. "Tristan, it's Brinkley. We're over. Bye."

When she closed her phone, she noticed she had a message. It was from her mom: "Brinkley, we've decided to stay an extra week. If you need anything, just use the credit card or ask Tallulah."

Brinkley deleted it and called Miranda. "I'm back," she said.

"How'd it go?"

"Well, let's just say that Joe Schlossman ended up in the ER, but he'll be fine."

"Whoa! What'd you do to him?"

Before Brinkley could answer, her phone beeped that a call was waiting. When she saw it was from Tristan, she rejected it and continued talking to Miranda. "I'll tell you about it when I see you at the play tonight."

"Won't your family flip out if they see you talking to me?"

"I just got a message from my mom. They're not coming."

"Brinkley . . . I'm sorry. I know you must be disappointed."

"Of course I'm disappointed. But it's OK, really," she said. "I'm just going to have to accept my parents for who they are and not take it personally. Besides, I'll be hanging out with you and Matt."

"Won't you be a little busy, what with being the star and all?"

"Not to worry," Brinkley said. "I've got it all figured out."

chapter thirty-seven

*A*fter everything that she'd been through, Brinkley was certain that she could play the part of Laura with integrity. She knew what it meant to understand someone else and to see things through another's eyes. She could bring to Laura a sincerity that would break the audience's hearts.

But she wouldn't.

Mr. Ellis would probably be thrilled to have Emma take over the part, despite the progress Brinkley had shown in the last rehearsals.

The only person who would be a problem was Emma Paulis.

When she got to the theater, Emma was already backstage. "I've got your wardrobe changes right here, in scene order," Emma told her. "Opening night, Brinkley! Isn't it exciting?"

"Wouldn't you be more excited if you were playing Laura tonight?" Brinkley asked.

"I'll have my chance someday," Emma said. "But I'm happy for you. I know you're going to be wonderful. You were so great in rehearsal yesterday!"

"Well, I guess I'll just go get a feel for the stage before the audience begins arriving. You know, just to calm those opening-night jitters."

"I always do that, too!" Emma said. "It really does help, doesn't it?"

"It's going to help tonight," Brinkley said. She walked out onto the stage, and, when no one was watching, sat down. Then she pounded the floor with her foot. "OW!" she screamed. "Oh, ow! Ow! Ow!"

Mr. Ellis, the cast, and the crew came rushing to her aid.

"Brinkley, are you all right?" Mr. Ellis asked.

"I'm afraid not," she replied. "My ankle—I think it's sprained!"

"Oh, no," Mr. Ellis said. "Do you think you can still go on tonight?"

"Try to walk on it, Brinkley," said Emma.

Brinkley made quite a show of wincing in pain as she tried to bear weight on her right leg. "I can't!" she wailed. "There's no way! Emma, you'll have to fill in for me."

"Are you sure you aren't up to it? Laura is supposed to be crippled, after all."

Brinkley cursed herself for not thinking of that. Why hadn't she faked a gastrointestinal virus? That was the kind of thing people were more than willing to take your word for without empirical evidence. "I just can't bear the pain," she said. "I'll probably have to take a painkiller, and I won't be able to remember my lines."

"Emma, I guess you'll have to step in," Mr. Ellis said. "Brinkley, I'm so sorry."

Brinkley pretended to put up a brave front. "The show must go on, Mr. Ellis. The show must go on."

"Why are you limping?" Matt asked when she met him in the lobby.

"I have to make it look good," she said.

"What?"

"Nothing. Emma's going on for me tonight. That's the way it should've been from the beginning. She deserved the part, not me."

"Brinkley, are you sure?"

"Absolutely," she replied. "Besides, I'd rather sit in the audience with you."

A woman turned around. "I couldn't help but overhear."

"Irirangi?" Brinkley asked. Then, to Matt, "Could you excuse us for just a second?"

"You were limping on the other side when you walked into the lobby," Irirangi said.

"Oh!" Brinkley said. "It's, uh . . . weird. My other foot hurts too, now."

"I know what you did, Brinkley."

"You do?"

"Yes. I know a lot of things about you that you don't think I know."

"Like what?"

"Like the kind of transformations you've been undergoing the past couple of weeks."

"Transformations?" Did she really know about the jumps, or was this metaphoric psychobabble?

"I once told you that an open mind is a beautiful thing," said Irirangi. "I believe your mind has been opened. As well as your heart." She handed her an envelope. "This is for your principal. Your therapy is complete. It was my privilege to know you, Brinkley Harper."

Just before she opened one of the doors to leave, Irirangi turned to Brinkley and said, "Remember to get enough rest. I think you'll find that you'll be sleeping better from now on."

"Who was that?" asked Matt.

"Irirangi," she said.

"Oh, interesting name." He typed it into his iPhone. "It comes from Maori culture and means 'spirit voice.' Cool."

Someone behind Brinkley asked, "Don't you need to get dressed for the play?"

"Tallulah! What are you doing here?"

"I didn't want to miss your big night," she said.

"Oh, I'm so sorry! There's been a change of plans. I'm not going to be in the play after all." Brinkley looked at Tallulah's purse. "That purse is severely lacking in yellowness and Tory Burchness! What gives?"

Tallulah blushed. "Oh, I didn't want to risk getting something on it. It's too expensive!"

Brinkley shook her finger at her. "Fabulous bags are meant to be carried, Tallulah! I see I'm going to have my work cut out for me with you!" She hugged her. "It means the world to me that you came. Come on. Let's go find some seats."

When Brinkley, Tallulah, and Matt walked into the theater, they passed Bette and a group of popular girls, who whispered and giggled at them. *Let them,* Brinkley thought. *Who cares?* She hadn't felt this good in weeks—maybe ever.

"Isn't that your best friend we just passed?" Matt asked.

"Bette? No. Bette is not my friend," she said. "*That* is my friend." She waved to Miranda, who came over to sit with them.

"So, I see you're back to your old self," Miranda said. "And I see you've made the loser list." She nodded towards Bette. "Looks like we have a new queen at Story."

Brinkley said, "I guess so."

"I don't think you'll be attending any more lake-house parties," Miranda said.

"All the more time for movie nights at my house," she said.

"So we're on for *The Godfather* trilogy?" asked Miranda.

"*The Godfather?* I love that movie!" Matt said.

"Great!" said Brinkley. "We'll invite Emma, Carly, Ivy, Jae . . . and Princess of Darkness, if you want."

Miranda asked, "Who?"

"Oh, I forgot to tell you about that." She leaned over toward Matt and whispered in his ear, "Maybe we could fix up one of your friends with Miranda?"

"Maybe," said Matt. "But not Joe. He already likes Carly."

"Seriously? That's excellent!" Brinkley said.

The curtain came up, and Tom Wingfield walked onstage, promising "truth in the pleasant disguise of illusion."

In the darkened auditorium, Brinkley took Matt's hand and rested her head on his shoulder. She yawned once and thought of how peacefully she'd sleep that night.

Acknowledgments

The author wishes to thank Susan Shapiro Barash for her knowledge of female behavior; Krutin Patel, who knows how to keep a plot moving; Tony Brusate for his knowledge of cars; and Ken Min, Yang Joo Min, and Soon Jin Kim for their help with the Korean translation.

Photo: Lynn Anderson

Ginger Rue has written for *Girls' Life, Teen Vogue,* and *Seventeen* magazines, and was the advice columnist for *Sweet 16.* Her first novel, *Brand-New Emily,* was published by Tricycle Press in 2009. She lives in Northport, Alabama.

Tricycle Press and the Tricycle Press colophon are registered trademarks
of Random House, Inc.

Library of Congress Cataloging-in-Publication Data
Rue, Ginger.
      Jump : a novel / by Ginger Rue. — 1st ed.
          p. cm.
      Summary: A bullying, narcissistic high school junior discovers the transforming
power of compassion when she literally "walks in someone else's shoes."
      [1. Compassion—Fiction. 2. Self-perception—Fiction. 3. Popularity—Fiction.
4. High schools—Fiction. 5. Schools—Fiction.] I. Title.
      PZ7.R88512Ju 2010
      [Fic]—dc22

                                                                              2010008877

      ISBN 978-1-58246-334-6 (hardcover)
      ISBN 978-1-58246-362-9 (Gibraltar lib. bdg.)

Printed in U.S.A.

Design by Katy Brown
Typeset in Adobe Garamond and Cruz Ballpoint

1 2 3 4 5 6 — 14 13 12 11 10

First Edition